The Last Fifth Grade of Emerson Elementary

Sydney

Rennie

Tyler

Norah

Rachel

Sloane

Mark

Ben

Katie

Gaby

Brianna

Edgar

Newt

George

Jason

Hannah

Shoshanna

Rajesh

To Nisha,

Make your voice heard!

THE LAST FIFTH GRADE OF

Emerson Elementary

LAURA SHOVAN

WENDY
LAMB
BOOKS

Text copyright © 2016 by Laura Shovan
Jacket and interior art copyright © 2016 by Abigail Halpin

Visit us on the Web! randomhousekids.com

Educators and librarians, for a variety of teaching tools, visit us at RHTeachersLibrarians.com

Library of Congress Cataloging-in-Publication Data
Title: The last fifth grade of Emerson Elementary / Laura Shovan.
Description: First edition. | New York : Wendy Lamb Books,
an imprint of Random House Children's Books, [2016].
Summary: "A story told in verse from multiple perspectives of the graduating fifth grade class of Emerson Elementary. The kids join together to try to save their school from being torn down to make way for a supermarket"
— Provided by publisher.
Identifiers: LCCN 2015026501 | ISBN 978-0-553-52137-5 (hardback) |
ISBN 978-0-553-52138-2 (lib. bdg.) | ISBN 978-0-553-52139-9 (ebook)
Subjects: | CYAC: Novels in verse. | Schools—Fiction. | BISAC: JUVENILE FICTION / Stories in Verse. | JUVENILE FICTION / School & Education.
Classification: LCC PZ7.5.S49 Las 2016 | DDC [Fic]—dc23

The text of this book is set in 13-point Blueprint.
Jacket design by Kate Gartner
Interior design by Trish Parcell

Printed in the United States of America
10 9 8 7 6 5 4 3
First Edition

For all of my students,
who have been my best teachers,
but especially Robbie and Julia.

"And they were all, when their
souls grew warm, poets."
—RAY BRADBURY

FIRST QUARTER

· · · · · · · · · · · ·

Yo, Notebook.
I am your poet.
I will fill you with words.
I don't mind writing
a poem for our teacher,
some rhymes
Ms. Hill will feature
in our fifth-grade book.
My whole class
is writing down
what happens this year,
but I won't frown.
I've got nothing to fear.
I'm already a poet.
My verses are off the hook.
Hey, Notebook,
hope you don't mind
waiting in my backpack.
I know you're hating
the dark in there.
Smells murky as old turkey.
Later today I'll take you out
in a sunny place, tell you
what life's all about
for a fifth-grade poet.
Fresh air, blue sky,
my notebook and I.

My name is George Washington Furst.
Don't laugh. My parents are history teachers.
They met at George Washington's house.
It's a museum called Mount Vernon.
Vernon is also the name of our cat,
who lives with me and my mom.
My dad doesn't live with us.
He moved out and took half the furniture,
so probably we won't visit Mount Vernon
on my birthday like usual
because nothing's like usual.
If Mount Vernon is still standing
after nearly three hundred years,
why do people want to demolish
Emerson Elementary?
School is the only place
I can count on to never change.
Maybe I'll run for class president.
If I'm elected, I'll tell our principal
that buildings can last hundreds of years.
Mrs. Stiffler has to listen
to the class president, right?
If I save our school,
maybe my dad will get it:
Some things are worth holding on to.

We only have 180 days
at Emerson Elementary.
When this school year ends,
I will have spent
one thousand days
in this building.
I want a thousand more
so I'll never have to say
goodbye to friends
like Sydney and Katie.
I wish Emerson
could be my school forever,
but everyone is talking
about a plan
to tear the building down.
Even if we write poems
about this year and save them
for the school time capsule,
it's going to be
like we were never here.
I wish fifth grade
wasn't such a tornado,
whirling and spinning,
everyone scattered
in different directions,
our school gone,
empty space
left behind.

August 28
• • • • • • •
THE LAST FIFTH GRADE
Sloane Costley

Walking into school in my brand-new clothes.
Last week of August, still got sunburn on my nose.
Checking out the little kids, I feel so tall.
Over summer, someone must've shrunk this hall.
Mom let me get lip gloss and some sparkly pens.
Sydney's backpack matches mine because we're twins.
I picked out exactly what we both should wear.
Yeah, we look alike, but you don't have to stare.
Did you hear the Board of Ed might sell our school?
Emerson could be a mall or something cool.
If they knock this place down, we should have a parade,
'cause no one else will ever be the last fifth grade.

My dad says if this school closes down,
we'll get to go somewhere better.
My mom's a major in the army.
She says the way to make things happen
is to take charge. So I'm stepping up,
being a leader. I got Shoshanna
and Brianna to help with my campaign.
Vote for me if you want to say goodbye
to bathroom doors that don't shut right,
sweating in classrooms with broken AC,
grungy windows, grimy desks,
basketball hoops without any nets.
I can't understand why so many people
want to save this run-down old building.
We deserve to go to school
someplace nice. It's our right!
Vote for me if you agree.

September 2

SCHOOL CLOTHES
Brianna Holmes

I am hot-pink loud
and no one sees
the holes that I cover
with embroidery.

I am sleek black boots
up past my knee.
No one knows they're plastic
and too big for me.

If a hem can be sewn,
you don't throw out the sweater.
Why tear down our school
when rebuilding is better?

I love hand-me-downs
and thrift-store jeans,
and I'm still stylish
as the fifth-grade queens.

Ms. Hill, do we have to start every morning
listening to folk music while we write poetry?
Writing is hard enough without "If I Had a Hammer"
pounding my head. In twenty-five years,
when some kid opens the time capsule
from our school, he's not going to care about me
or my poems. Why can't our class
do a cool project? The fourth grade
is making a photo album for the time capsule.
You could even put in that picture you love,
the one on your desk where you look like a total hippie.
Writing is worse than washing the dishes.
It's worse than taking out the trash.
Ms. Hill, don't you ever have a day
when you don't have anything
to say?

September 4
• • • • • • • •
THEN AND NOW
Shoshanna Berg

When my sister moved up
from fifth grade,
I stood right here,
so little I held my mom's hand.
All the Emerson teachers
waited near the glass hallway
that connects our school
to Montgomery Middle.
On the other side,
the middle-school teachers
were ready for their new students.
My sister lined up with her class.
I remember her yellow sundress.
When the fifth graders
stepped into the bright hallway,
all the teachers clapped.
Goodbye, goodbye!
As they crossed from elementary
into middle school,
the teachers on the other side
clapped a welcome.
Isn't it funny? The one thing
I'm looking forward to
about fifth grade
is how it ends.

Every time
I try to write a poem,
the pencil goes
scritch a scratch.

My pencils
tick a tack
drumbeats
on my desk.

My feet *boom*
badoom the floor
like a heartbeat
always moving.

My words
take up a rhythm
like the wind
blowing outside.

Scritch a scratch
Tick a tack
Boom badoom
Outside outside

How can I write
when everything around
makes an interesting
sound?

PING-PONG RIFF
Jason Chen

I have to write a poem for a class project?
My brain bounces around for ideas,
but it's not like a Ping-Pong ball,
going back and forth in straight lines.
(Not all Asians play Ping-Pong.
I play football, and also
saxophone.) A poem?
My brain bounces back to summer,
hurling insults during Shakespeare camp.
Thou deboshed fish!
How couldst thou require our class
to compose verses every quarter?
Didst thou say every quarter?
My brain bounces from Shakespearean curses
to quarter notes, filling up a page of sheet music.
Soon, I'm bebopping a jazz rhythm.
Words begin to flow from my pencil
like notes from a saxophone.
Finally, my brain starts riffing.

Every morning I braid my hair for school.
Sometimes I use the lemon oil my sister gave me.
I rub a drop into my hair.
The smell reminds me of when I was little,
the lemon tree in my grandfather's courtyard.
I call him Jaddi. He is not Grandpa.

Every morning I walk to school.
There is a path through the woods.
I follow Ben and his father.
They look for mushrooms and insects
while I gaze up at the trees, so tall.
There are no trees like this
where I come from, Jerusalem,
but there are also no gold autumn leaves,
no bare branches sprouting in spring.
If they demolish our school,
I hope they leave these trees alone.
I love how cool their shade feels
even though the days are hot.

Every morning, Ms. Hill tells us
we must write in our journals.
In June we will have a record
of our fifth-grade year
to put inside the school time capsule.
Before I write a poem, I talk to myself in Arabic.
In Arabic, the words sound like a river
flowing over rocks, jagged and smooth.
I hear Jaddi's voice.
English isn't good enough for telling poems.
It sounds like knives and forks
clanking in a drawer.

Everything's bigger in Texas.
That's what they say where I'm from,
but folks in the Lone Star State
never seen Ms. Hill.
She should've been called Ms. Mountain.
Just about the tallest teacher I ever met.
Her hair isn't dull gray
but silvery, and shiny as the trumpet
I've been bugging my mom about.
Kids say Ms. Hill's strict, scolds the girls
in our class who can't stay friends
more than two days in a row,
not like me and Mark.
My first day at Emerson Elementary,
Ms. Hill asked Mark to be my buddy.
How'd Ms. Hill know we'd be friends?
Does she have a Magic 8 Ball hidden
behind that old black-and-white picture—
our teacher, younger than my mom,
scarf wrapped around her hair,
marching in a big parade?
Kids say Ms. Hill is going to retire.
If the school goes down,
she'll go down with it.
But having her for my fifth-grade teacher
almost makes me glad
my family moved north.

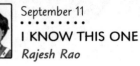
I raise my hand.
I say, "Ooh! Ooh!
I know this one."
I stand up, too.

I wave and groan.
I stomp my feet.
She tells me to
please take my seat.

My arm is tired.
Please call on me!
I want to speak.
Why can't she see?

She's giving someone
else a chance.
I wasted my
right-answer dance.

At home, my mom says
I could argue a tiger out of its own stripes.
I act like I'm a brave tiger
for my little sister Phoenix when I walk her
to first grade every morning.
But as soon as I say goodbye
I'm more like a rabbit, small and quiet,
wanting to blend in.
Phoenix is real shy. She won't like it
if they sell our elementary and middle school.
What if we get split up next year?
She'll have no sister Rennie to walk with.

I hear everyone complaining
about plans to tear down Emerson,
but nobody's doing a thing about it.
Except George.
He's going to change things up,
run for student council
and save our school.
I'm going to tell George
he needs a vice president
and I volunteer.
I'm done being a rabbit.
I will stand up tall and argue.
I will roar like a tiger until someone
hears what I have to say.

September 16
• • • • • • • •
MY NAME
Sydney Costley

I used to like my name,
until second grade,
when we moved to this school.
Jason Chen thought it was funny
to call me Sydney Kidney
and my twin Sloane the Clone.

I used to like how our names
aren't too fancy.
But my best friend
is Rachel Chieko Stein,
and her name is really pretty.

I used to like how my name
has so many letter Ys
because my dad said
my name made me "wise."
But now I am older.
So many things are changing,
I think I am full of *whys* instead . . .

like why does the Board of Ed
want to close Emerson?
Why do they want to split up our class?
And why does everyone but me
want to spend three more years
going to this school?

Poems that have rules.
Counting word beats in three lines
makes sense to my brain.

Little white frogs live
along our school's back brick wall.
Look inside my hand!

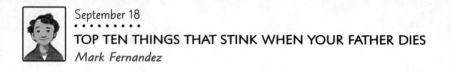

TOP TEN THINGS THAT STINK WHEN YOUR FATHER DIES
Mark Fernandez

1. You can't sleep.

2. You watch late-night TV.

3. You start acting like a talk-show host.

4. Everyone but the new kid thinks you're weird.

5. They all ignore you.

6. There's no one to hang around with,
   so you miss your dad.

7. The moms in your neighborhood feel bad for you.

8. They make their kids invite you places.

9. You think you have friends.

10. You don't.

My mother asked me to be nice to Mark,
invite him to the movies with a friend.
She said, "No one will see you in the dark,
and if they do, the world's not going to end!"
My mother doesn't know that Hannah Wiles
judges everything I do and say.
She tells me who's my friend and what's in style,
and when we're out at recess what we'll play.
So I took Gaby with me to make sure
no one would say I asked Mark on a date.
They ate my popcorn. I went to buy more,
and there was Hannah, outside Theater 8.
I hid inside the bathroom for an hour.
I wish I could break free from Hannah's power.

"EL PALOMITO"
Gaby Vargas

Espero el viernes la semana entera.
¡La clase de música!
Cuando canto, muestro cómo me siento
alegre, triste.
Cuando canto, mis palabras
suenan claras, fuertes.
Pero cuando hablo inglés,
me enredo. Intento decirle a Shoshanna,
"Mark es cómico, siempre está bromeando,
pero sus ojos marrón son tristes
y esconden cosas que no quiere decir."
Intento escribir primero las palabras
¡pero escribir en inglés es aun más difícil!
Buscar palabras
en mi diccionario inglés-español
toma demasiado tiempo.

No encuentro las palabras correctas
para decirle a Mark, "Siento mucho lo de tu papá."
Así que le enseño a tocar "El Palomito,"
una canción triste de mi país,
yo cantando y Mark con su guitarra.

I wait all the week for Friday,
the class of music!
When I sing, I show how I feel
happy, sad.
When I sing, my words
sound clear and strong.
But when I talk English
I make a mistake.
I want to tell to Shoshanna,
"Mark is funny, he always jokes,
but his brown eyes
cover things he don't say."
I intend to write the words first,
but to write in English is more difficult!
To look for words
in my English and Spanish dictionary
is too much time.

I don't find correct words
to say to Mark, "I am sorry for your father."
So I teach to him to play *"El Palomito,"*
a sad song of my country.
I sing and Mark plays his guitar.

September 23
• • • • • • • •
CHANGES
George Furst

It's strange how things change
but also kind of stay the same.
I'm still my parents' favorite (only) kid,
and we're still a family, even though
my dad has his own apartment.
I still ride the school bus every day.
We take the same route, but the horse farm
we used to pass in first grade
is an apartment building now.

I know there must be other kids like me
at our school, who need a place
that never changes. Because parents split up,
best friends move to a big house across town
and you never hear from them again,
but Emerson Elementary is always here.
It drips and leaks. The gym floor is cracked.
The walls could use some paint,
but all our school needs is a little fixing up.

Change is happening all around Emerson.
That's why we have to show Mrs. Stiffler
and the Board of Ed it wouldn't take much
to keep our school from changing.
Just like I have to show my father
it wouldn't take much
to put our family back together.

It's writing time again?
Some mornings
my words are clumsy.
They bump into each other.
Smoosh
      boosh
           BAM!
They've got as much rhythm
as an octopus
doing the chicken dance.
Some mornings
after we say the Pledge,
my words are still
crawling out of bed.
They've got
fuzzy slippers on.
They haven't
brushed their teeth.
P.U.
This poem stinks.

September 26
· · · · · · · · · ·
LUCKY HAT
Ben Kidwell

Blue,
my favorite color,
pin-striped like the Yankees,
my favorite baseball team. The bill
is perfectly broken in, just the right
amount of curve to it. My mom promised
not to wash it, ever. Dust and sweat from
my winning games. I didn't know hats are
not allowed during spelling tests. I swear I
wasn't cheating. Ms. Hill, please give me back my lucky hat.

No matter how many times I tell my sister
appearances MATTER,
she still dresses like some
Olympic soccer coach
might call her any second
so she'd better be ready to play NOW.
Suddenly, it's a miracle!
Sydney's paying attention,
asking me which teachers are stylish.
The young ones, duh!
No offense, Ms. Hill,
but I have seen the old photo
on your desk, and even when
you were young in the 1970s
that paisley scarf you wore
wasn't exactly fashionable.
Last week, Sydney asked our mom
to take her to the mall.
Gasp! Have all my fashion lectures,
the pictures from *Vogue*
I taped on our bedroom wall,
finally gotten through to her?
There is a chance we might be popular
if we dress cool and go to a new middle school
(where no one calls me Sloane the Clone).
When Sydney came home from shopping,
I inspected her bags.

A denim skirt, purple tie-dyed T-shirt,
and cute navy blue Vans. Wow.
"Well?" Sydney said
when she tried on her outfit for me.
"Finally," I said, "you look like a girl."

This is why I don't like skirts.
It feels weird when I walk.
These shoes hurt my feet.
I wanted to look pretty. But I'm not.
I thought a purple shirt would be okay,
but I look like an exploding grape soda
or a purple blob,
and it's not even Halloween yet.
Why did I try to be
not me
on Picture Day?

October 1
• • • • • • •
PICTURE DAY
Jason Chen

When I leave the house
   my hair is gelled,
   my shirt is pressed,
   my teeth are brushed,
   my mom's impressed.
   I look so nice
   I want to spew
   my Cheerios
   on someone's shoe.

When it's time for pictures
   my hair's in spikes,
   my shirt's all loose,
   my teeth are pink
   from drinking juice.
   I look so bad
   I want to hurl
   my lunch upon
   some dressed-up girl.

Yesterday
my father came home
to help me and my mom
make election posters.
They say
"Make Furst Your First Choice"
and "SOS—Save Our School."

After dinner, we sat
at the kitchen table
like we used to.
My mom drew the letters
with blue marker.
My dad added red glitter.
I stuck pictures of my face
inside the big letter O.

I used so much glue,
I thought we'd be stuck
at that table
forever.

October 3
• • • • • • •
ELECTION DAY
Norah Hassan

Everyone is excited!
Listen carefully while Ms. Hill explains how we
Elect our student council.
Candidates must sign up by Friday. George wants me
To run for secretary.
I can help him save our school because I am
Organized and
Neat.

Does one election make me feel like
A real American?
Yes!

He moves real slow,
like one of those giant
hundred-year-old
tortoises at the zoo.
He is brown, always
smiling, never down.
Has wrinkled
tortoise-neck skin.
He remembers when
my father
went to this school.
He frowns
when I tell him
they're going to crash it
to the ground.
So what
if Emerson's
getting old?

Grandpa talks to me
in a voice low
and smooth.

"I've seen you
from my window,"
he'll say.
"Climbing trees
the way I used to do,
sitting in the branches,
telling yourself
stories." I wish
Grandpa was
a kid again. I think
we would be friends.

At Hannah's father's house I saw a piano.
She called it a baby grand.
Looked full-grown to me.

Rennie's house has its own library.
Books on every wall
and soft chairs to read in.

I went to Sloane and Sydney's.
They have their own walk-in closet filled with clothes.
Some still have price tags on them.

Shoshanna's got this little box on her door.
She says it has a prayer inside. At the motel where I live,
we can't put stuff on our door.

If they close our school in June,
maybe the kids in my class will get it . . .
what it's like to be homeless.

Until then, I want to play at each girl's house
so when my mom gets a job, an apartment,
I'll know exactly what I want:

A place filled with music and books,
closets stuffed with the clothes I design,
and my own room—the answer to my prayers.

GREEN TOENAILS
Katie McCain

I like to paint my toenails green.
It drives my mother crazy.
My room's a mess. Mom wants it neat.
She says that I am lazy.
I streaked my hair with blue Kool-Aid.
I stand out in a crowd.
Mom says I'm like my own parade
because I am so loud.

My grades are good. My friends are nice.
I sing and dance and juggle.
Mom would have liked a quiet kid,
who never gets in trouble.
I'm noisy, goofy, colorful,
and I'm okay with that.
Still, my mother seems to think
her daughter is a brat.

I have Asperger's.
My aide is Mr. Ron White.
He says I am smart.
He helps me write down poems.
It is hard to describe things.

October 10
· · · · · · · ·
OBSTACLE COURSE
Rachel Chieko Stein

The best thing we do all year in P.E.
is the obstacle course.
I love climbing on the gym bars
that curve like a rainbow.
I can do it, no hands.
At home, we have lots of equipment
for my brother Alex.
He's in middle school,
but he doesn't go next door
to Montgomery Middle.
Alex uses a wheelchair
and a scooter to get around,
so every place we go
is an obstacle course.
We're hoping he gets strong enough
to walk by himself,
just with crutches.
Some kids with disabilities
go to our school,
but not Alex.
Maybe if they close Emerson
and Montgomery Middle,
Alex and I will be able to go
to the same school,
and Alex could be in PE
with so-called normal kids
and be better than all of them
at the obstacle course.

When your last name
is Fernandez
everyone thinks
you're automatically
fluent in Spanish.
My dad was always telling me
and my older sisters
¡habla español!
And we'd say, Papi, no way.
They'll stick us
in some kind of ESL class.

So I'm helping Gaby
rewrite her poems in English.
We both need the practice
and I like having someone
to speak Spanish with.
I miss the sound
now my dad's not around.

MY SONG
Tyler La Roche

New kid, new kid,
what's your name?
Are you cool
or are you lame?
Wild as a bear
or calm and tame?
New kid, new kid, new kid.

Big guy, sky high,
where you from?
Mansion, farm,
or city slum?
Are you smart
or are you dumb?
New kid, new kid, new kid.

Red head, white bread,
Why are you here?
Your lunch smells funny
and your accent's weird.
How about you
disappear?
New kid, new kid, new kid.

Draw her posters.
Write her speech.
Give her my skirt to wear.

Buy a new
red, white, and blue
headband for her hair.

At recess
I find every girl,
go up to them and say,

"You better vote
for Hannah Wiles
when it's Election Day."

I know that she
won't do a thing
to help our school survive.

She sees herself
as the queen bee,
and I'm part of her hive.

When Hannah wins
class president
I'll finally be free.

If she is boss
of our whole grade
she won't be bossing me.

October 16
• • • • • • • •
ELECTION DAY
Rajesh Rao

The teacher asks me to be
an impartial judge on Election Day.
She also asks me to clean the board,
log in the class computers,
help Newt find his pencils,
sit by kids who get in trouble,
be the Captain of Patrols.
She says I'm a good influence.
She calls me "responsible."
Maybe I should have run.
Instead I'm counting votes
for Hannah and George.
Don't worry.
I'm too responsible to tell anyone
when the kids on George's
Save Our School ticket
win by a landslide.

Shoshanna says
I always
have to get my way.
That is so not true.
If I always got my way
I would have won
the class election.
If I always got my way
I would've been picked
for safety patrols
instead of Rachel Stein.
If I always got my way
my parents would still
be married, I wouldn't
have a stepmother and
two annoying half brothers.
If I always got my way
I wouldn't have to go
live with my father
for the rest
of the school year.
If Shoshanna
weren't so mad at me
I'd tell her,
if I always got my way
my mother wouldn't be
deploying.

Why did my mom sign up to chaperone?
I'll have to answer questions like "Who's she?"
"Your mom is white?" Well, should I be a clone
with her light hair and skin, not brown like me?
I'll slide down in my seat and read a book,
so kids won't stare at us the whole bus ride.
I hate when they're pretending not to look.
My mom is cool. Why should I have to hide?
So what if I am black and also white?
Who cares that I don't look just like my mom?
My family is different, but we're tight.
Get over it, because there's nothing wrong.
If someone gets up in my face today,
at least that's what I think I'm going to say.

So my mother,
who chaperones
EVERYTHING,
had to come
to the Newseum.
And the one thing
she wanted me
(and Sydney, Tyler,
Mark, and Gaby)
to see was photos
from some famous
Women's Liberty March
in Washington, DC.
Because my crazy
hippie grandmother
was there,
doing embarrassing
inappropriate stuff
like lighting fire
to her underwear.
And I'm looking close,
trying to spot Nana,
when Tyler says, "Hey!"
And he points to a face
in a photograph.

There is a girl
in a paisley scarf,
turning around to scream
at the policeman
handcuffing her.
And Tyler says,
"It looks a lot like
that old picture
of Ms. Hill."

Sloane took a picture.
She sent the picture to Hannah
with a text: *Is this Ms. Hill?*
Hannah sent it to Shoshanna,
who forwarded it to Jason,
who showed it to Edgar and Raj.
Soon our whole class was crowded
in front of a single photograph
at the Newseum. We've all seen
the picture on Ms. Hill's desk.
It must have been taken the same day,
when she marched for women's rights
in Washington, DC.
Ms. Hill is always telling us
to make our voices heard.
We are starting to get the message.

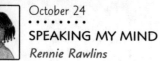

October 24

SPEAKING MY MIND

Rennie Rawlins

Dear Ms. Hill,

The whole class is talking
about the picture on your desk
where you're standing on the steps
of Capitol Hill.

The whole class is saying
you were really brave,
speaking your mind
to the government.
But the whole class is saying
we're just fifth graders.
Who's going to listen to us?

I say, yes, we *are* fifth graders.
We should stand up
for the younger kids at this school,
like my sister Phoenix.
I promised her I'd do whatever it takes
so she could stay at Emerson next year
and I'd be right next door
at Montgomery Middle.

Maybe it's true,
a bunch of fifth graders
have no say about what happens
to our school, but
in fifth grade we're supposed to be
studying democracy
and constitutional rights,
right?
Well, I already know
the First Amendment
is the right to free speech.

Your student,
Rennie

Ms. Hill,
we won't tell anyone
you got arrested.
It was a long time ago,
and Rennie, Norah, and I know
it's okay to get locked up
for something
you believe in,
like civil rights.

Ms. Hill,
I promised to
Save Our School
if I got to be
student council president,
but I don't know how.
My dad hasn't been
around much lately,
and my mom's busy,
so I can't ask them for ideas.

And since you
marched in Washington,
even though it was
a long time ago,
we were hoping, Rennie
and Norah and me,
your fifth-grade student council,
that you could teach us
how to tell the Board of Ed
we want to keep Emerson.

Ms. Hill,
a long time ago
you wanted the people in charge
to hear your ideas.
That's what we want
now.

HIJAB
Norah Hassan

On my birthday, there was a package
at our front door, covered in colorful stamps!
My cousin Amina sent it from Paris,
where she goes to college.
Inside was a head scarf, blue as a clear sky
woven with golden threads.
I wrapped the scarf around my face,
the way my mother does
when she puts on her hijab before work.
My older sister, whose clothes come
from Abercrombie & Fitch, said,
"You're not going to WEAR it. Like, outside?"
My cousin's letter said
there are laws in France forbidding girls
to wear a hijab at school.
This morning, when I put the hijab on,
I thought of you, Ms. Hill.
Even though you can't help us protest
to save Emerson, I want to say
thank you for marching for our rights
all those years ago. Including my right
to wear a head scarf at school.
Did you know then that you
would grow up to be a teacher?
When I put the hijab on
I float inside my scarf's blue cloth,
the golden threads shimmer
like sunshine on water.

Is it true
the Board of Ed wants to turn our school
into a supermarket?

That's what my mom heard
at Mrs. Stiffler's community meeting
last night.

Shelves of cereal
and toilet paper
instead of shelves of books.

Bored cashiers at the checkout
instead of the school media specialist
saying, "I've got a great book for you!"

Trucks filled
with tomatoes and broccoli
instead of buses filled with children.

I told George and Norah
it's time. The student council
needs to come up with a plan.

We can't let a bunch of vegetables
get in the way
of saving our school.

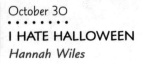

I HATE HALLOWEEN
Hannah Wiles

I wish I had a long black dress,
a bright green wig, and spider rings.
I wish I had a witch's broom
and other evil things.

I can't wear a tall black hat.
I'd be grounded for a week!
Our pastor says good kids do not
like to trick-or-treat, so

I don't draw pumpkins with a grin
or help my friends put makeup on.
The school parades, but I stay in.
I'm done with Halloween.

Our teacher's all dressed up
as this Emerson dude
who wrote about nature
and the things that he viewed.
He was walking in the sunshine.
He was swimming in the sea.
He was drinking up fresh air
and writing poetry.
Ralph Waldo was a poet.
Never heard of him before,
but his name's right there
on our school's front door.

SECOND QUARTER

ONE SEAT, TWO SEATS, WE HAVE NEW SEATS

Jason "Seuss" Chen

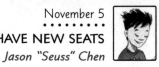

One seat, two seats, we have new seats.
Black seats, blue seats, missing-screw seats.

Some kids are glad and some are sad.
You sit by Teacher. Were you bad?

The teacher moved our chairs, but why?
I don't know. Go ask a fly!

Some seats are comfy, some are hard.
I wish my seat were in the yard.

Oh me! Oh my! I want to cry!
I'm still by Katie. That's no lie.

Some girls are sporty. Some are brainy.
I'm next to one who is complainy.

Why wasn't I moved? I cannot say.
I'd rather sit far, far away.

I wish I sat by someone new.
If you were I, what would you do?

November 6
• • • • • • • •
A LIMERICK
Katie McCain

There once was a girl named McCain,
who sat next to someone insane.
He thought it was cool
to act like a fool,
but his poems gave her a migraine.

I
don't
want to
revise this
poem. I like it.
These are the words my brain thought of
when our class learned about the Fibonacci sequence.

I
like
my school,
Emerson
Elementary.
If bulldozers demolish it,
how will everyone at my new school know who I am?

November 10
· · · · · · · · · ·
OPPOSITE POEM
Hannah Wiles

At my mom's house it's just us girls.
Calm and quiet. Nice and neat.
Our Friday-night tradition is
movies and manicures.
Shoshanna usually sleeps over.
My mom gets up early
(she calls it an old army habit)
and makes banana french toast.
Shoshanna and I wash the dishes.

At my dad's house
it's a chaos of little boys
crashing and bashing.
Every night someone cries
over a bump or a bruise,
a toy or lost shoes.
Shoshanna won't come over.
She says it's too loud,
toys scattered everywhere.
And sharing a bathroom
with two younger brothers?
Don't get me started.

The first time I got to sleep over
at my dad's new apartment
I asked him a history question:
When the people (meaning me)
don't agree with decisions
the government (meaning him)
is making, how can those people
tell the leaders they are unhappy?
He thought about my question
while he cooked our spaghetti
because my dad can't take a hint.
Then he said, "A good first step
is writing a petition."
So I wrote a petition to my parents,
explaining that I should get a vote
when they make decisions
about our family, but
I don't have any brothers and sisters.
Can a petition work
when it only has one signature?

INDOOR RECESS

Edgar Lee Jones

I don't want to play chess
with Raj today. I've got
the best beanbag chair
in the reading corner and a book
to make the rain disappear.
In this chapter, the hero
is galloping across sunny fields.
(What are Rennie and George
whispering about
and why can't they do it
somewhere else?)
I keep reading, find out
the hero is a king in disguise.
(I hope they don't
ask me to play cards.
He's about to save the kingdom!)
I want to see how my book ends,
but Rennie moves closer,
says I'm the best writer in our class.
She and George and Norah
need my help. (I don't know
how to write a petition.
Why can't they go away?)
Can't they see
I want to be
alone with my book?

During math, I'm like a dog
that wants to play outside
but no one will open the door.
I can't hold still. I feel itchy.
I look at the trees through the window,
toss something at Sydney's desk.
Want to play? She shakes her head.
I bite my nails, chew erasers,
look out the window.
Green grass. Bare branches.
Will they still be here next year?
I tap my feet, click my teeth,
dream up stories about dogs
living wild behind a supermarket.
I can almost see
yellow eyes out there, near the trees.
They're looking back at me.

RALPH WALDO EMERSON
Rachel Chieko Stein

I can picture Ralph Waldo Emerson
the way you described him, Ms. Hill . . .
wandering through the forest,
looking at trees and birds,
feeling like he's part
of something big.
Sometimes I see Ben
walking near the edge of the woods
at recess. I told Sydney
Ben must be a poet,
in love with nature
like Ralph Waldo Emerson.
Sydney said I am crazy
and that no one understood
the poem you read to us today.
But when I listened
to Ralph Waldo Emerson's words,
my ears heard a river bubbling,
and wind rustling the branches
of a tall old tree. I think
when Ben isn't paying attention
he must be hearing
the river and the wind
like Ralph Waldo Emerson.

WHO DO YOU LIKE?
Sydney Costley

My friend
passed me a note
during Technology.
It said, "Who do you like?"
in purple pen.

Over the letter *i*
she put a heart
instead of a dot.

I wrote back, "Why?"
I like the same kids
as always. I like
you.

She wrote,
"Don't you wish
you were in love
like Gaby & Mark?"

I pressed the note flat
against my jeans.
I looked at my friend
and shook my head.
No.
Not like Gaby and Mark.

She pulled the note away.
My hand felt hot
where her fingers touched.
She wrote with her purple pen
and gave me back the note.

"Top-secret.
I like someone.
He is in our class."
I threw her note away.

When my mom came to school
for Special Person's Day
I was so happy!
Everyone in fifth grade was staring
at her uniform. They said "Wow!"
when I told them she's going overseas.
My mom noticed Norah
didn't have any family to sit with,
and next thing I knew the two of them
were speaking Arabic together.
My mom is a linguist.
Norah was sad that her parents
had to work today, but
she had a big smile on her face
after she talked to my mom.
When my mom left, she said goodbye
to Norah and told Shoshanna
she'd miss our Friday nights together.
(She doesn't know we're not getting along.)
Everyone calls her Major
except me. On Special Person's Day
I felt lucky because only I
get to call her Mom.

November 19
· · · · · · · · ·
MY NAME IS THE ROCK
Tyler La Roche

My name is La Roche.
That means "The Rock,"
so maybe my ancestors lived on one.
But The Rock could also mean rock music.
When our band practices,
Mark's guitar goes *wrow wrow,*
Ben's drumsticks beat *tick tick crash,*
Jason's sax sings *bebop bebop,*
Raj's fingers skid across the piano keys,
and I've got my trumpet
bap-bah bap-bah da da.
We need a cool name for the talent show.
I said we should be the La Roche Band,
because that means "The Rock Band."
Jason thinks we should call the band
Zoo Creatures and wear animal masks.
I'm fine with that. At school,
I'm still the new kid. Hardly anyone
knows me, which means
I can be anything. Even
a trumpet-playing buffalo.

My whole family was sitting in the cafeteria.
Aunts, uncles, cousins, even my grandparents.
My three sisters were the first act.
When they came onstage
their ankle bells and costumes looked
too bright for our worn-out school.
The music started.
I've heard it a million times.
They are always practicing
classical Indian dance at home
and at their Kathak class.
My sisters moved their hands
as if they wanted everyone to come closer
and listen to the folktale their dance tells.

I wanted to be in the talent show, too.
I wanted to play piano for Mark's band.
But my parents didn't want me to spend
so much time at Jason's house,
practicing rock music.
"Homework first," Dad always tells me.
"It's different for sons."

21 Noviembre
· · · · · · · · · ·
EL DUETO
Gaby Vargas

Sin un amigo
¡el escenario vacío se veía tan grande!
La cafetería está llena de asientos.
Las familias vienen al talent show.
Se me acelera el corazón,
un colibrí listo para volar.
Las luces del escenario están calientes,
pero Mark está a mi lado con su guitarra.
Se ve guapo con camisa blanca y corbata.
El pelo lo tiene engominado y en punta.
Lo veo hacerle señas a su mamá.
Eso es lindo también.
Me aliso la falda con manos temblorosas.
Mark toca las primeras notas.
Escucho a Mark tocar la canción que le enseñé.
Respiro hondo.
Empiezo a cantar.

Without a friend
the empty stage looks very big!
The cafeteria is full of seats.
The families come to the talent show.
My heart beats fast,
a hummingbird going to fly.
The lights of the stage are hot,
but Mark is to my side with his guitar.
Looks cute with white shirt and tie.
He has his hair with gel. It is pointy.
I see him make signs to his mom.
That is cute also.
I smooth my skirt. My hands tremble.
Mark touches the strings.
I hear Mark play the song I teach him.
I breathe deep.
I begin to sing.

November 24
• • • • • • • • •
LEFT OUT
Rajesh Rao

Edgar was my friend.
We shared a seat on the bus,
played chess at recess.

Now he's always with George Furst,
working on secret projects.

My family's Thanksgiving tradition was
after the guests were all gone
my father took me camping, just me and him.
Even in November, it was warm by the campfire.
The firelight made shadows.
Papi told stories about growing up
with Tio Carlos and Tio Dan,
the pranks they played on each other.
When we camped, my dad always made pancakes.
They tasted of smoke from the fire
even when I drenched them in syrup.

This year, my mom is taking me and my sisters
to Disney World over Thanksgiving break.
Tyler says I'm lucky, but I'm not.
Riding roller coasters and meeting Mickey Mouse
won't make me feel less sad
about Thanksgiving without my father.
No matter where I am, when I look up at the sky,
if I see stars, *las estrellas,* in the dark
I will remember camping with my dad.

HOW TO MAKE A MR. STICK GUY FLIP BOOK
Jason Chen

For Mark

Find a pack of sticky notes.
Think of a story starring
Mr. Stick Guy
and his Misadventures of Mayhem.
How about …
Mr. Stick Guy rides his skateboard.
Oh, no! He ollies right off a cliff
and lands on a giant cactus.
Thorns stick out of his stick butt.
Or …
Mr. Stick Guy fires a cannon at
Other Stick Guy (OSG for short).
OSG says, "Ouch!"
Or my favorite …
Mr. Stick Guy and OSG
in "The Bulldozer Battle."

Draw Mr. Stick Guy on the bottom
of a sticky note. Make sure
he's only as tall as your thumbnail.
Draw him again on the next page,
and again, and again.
Every time, change his stick arms and legs
a little bit. Use up every page
of the sticky pad, but save the big crash
for the last sheet.
Flip through the pages under your desk.
Laugh!
Don't get caught.

This Activity Is Appropriate Only for Recess.
—The Management

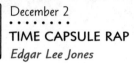

TIME CAPSULE RAP

Edgar Lee Jones

Hey, me from the future!
This is a message from me,
the kid you used to be,
known as Eddie Jones,
and sometimes Edgar Lee.
Do folks in the future
call you Mr. Jones,
Mr. Grown-Up,
Suit-Wearing Jones?
How tall are those
grown-up bones?

Hey, me from the future!
This is a message from me
on a time capsule ride,
years flash by in warp drive
and I'm coming to you live
from (count 'em) twenty-five
years in your past.
I want spoilers, man.
I've got to know my own story.
Am I quiet and shy?
Do I chase fame and glory?

Hey, me from the future!
This is a message from me.
When the time capsule's opened,
who will you see
in my fifth-grade poetry?
A stranger, a reader,
a poet, a brain?
Will you forget who I was
or stay just the same?
If I don't help
write that petition,
will it be
something I'm sorry for
when you're
future me?

Ms. Hill,
I'm glad you're the only one
who reads our poems.
Maybe a stranger will read them
in twenty-five years when they open
the time capsule, but I'll be old by then.
I like being able to write private stuff
and know that you are listening.
Does anyone in our class
write about what makes them happy?
I love running and swimming.
I love my dog, Shaggy. He runs and swims, too.
I love sunny days and going to the beach
with my sister and Rachel.
I think if you put our poems up in the hallway
the way you do with our other writing projects,
people would write poems about stupid stuff
like going to the mall and eating ice cream.
My favorite flavor is cookie dough.
I bet you like butter pecan.
Old-fashioned and kind of nutty.
Thanks for letting us write about
whatever we want in our poems.
Thanks for listening.

When it's warm out
my mom drops me
at the playground
before school.
She can't afford
to miss her morning class.
There's parents chatting,
kids playing.
Someone always
watches out for me
until the first bell rings.

When it's cold,
Mom drops me off
in the library
before school.
Rennie's mother
volunteers there
every morning.
I love shelving books
with Rennie
and her little sister Phoenix.
When we're done
Mrs. Rawlins lets us read
anything we want.

Some cold mornings
I pretend we all live together
in the library.
Rennie and Phoenix
are my sisters,
and Mrs. Rawlins
is my real mom.

Some mornings I like to watch
the middle schoolers
go in their separate door
when I walk my sister Phoenix
into Emerson.

My mother says hold tight
to Phoenix's hand.
Don't let her hear
the big kids cussing.
Don't let her see
the big kids kissing.

Sometimes I wonder why
Montgomery Middle students
don't say anything
about saving their school,
saving both our schools.

My mother says they're too busy
cussing and kissing,
too busy being middle schoolers
to help us. We may share a building,
but we've got two different doors.

MACMESS: AN EXPERIMENT IN POLLUTION
Jason "The Fifth-Grade Bard" Chen

A science classroom.
In the middle, a plastic bowl frothing.
Laughter.
Enter the four Lab Partners.

HANNAH: Three cups of water from the tap.
BEN: Three spoons of coffee, mixed clockwise.
KATIE: Ms. Hill calls—pour in Kool-Aid!
JASON: Stir it round our plastic bowl,
in the pencil shavings throw.
Make this water look polluted.
Add more gunk and don't dilute it.

ALL: Double, double, science trouble,
water churn and Kool-Aid bubble.

HANNAH: Ms. Hill's got a fish-shaped sponge
to drop in our liquid grunge.
BEN: Put the sponge fish in our cup.
KATIE: How much junk will get soaked up?
JASON: Stir the sponge fish round and round.
It's stuck in the coffee grounds.

ALL: Double, double, science trouble,
water churn and Kool-Aid bubble.

JASON: Why should we stick to our list?
        Experiments should have a twist.
        Piece of shrimp swiped from Ben's lunch.
        Apple core and Nestlé Crunch.
        Now our water's looking foul.
        Whoops! I need a paper towel.
HANNAH: Ugh. There's potion on my dress.
        Jason, you are such a mess.
KATIE: Hannah, Jason didn't do it.
        You grabbed the spoon and almost threw it.

ALL: Double, double, science trouble,
        water churn and Kool-Aid bubble.

JASON: Clean our desks off carefully.
        (Katie M. was nice to me.)

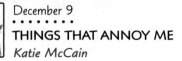

December 9

THINGS THAT ANNOY ME

Katie McCain

Jokes about vomit—too lame to laugh at.
Anyone who quotes Shakespeare at me.
Sitting next to a boy who chews pencils.
Odd habits like making flip
    books where people get squashed by a bulldozer.
Not being allowed to change my seat.

Calculator borrowers—get your own!
Hamster lovers (snakes are way better pets).
Everyone saying someone's crushing on me.
Nachos ... kidding! I love nachos. Names that start with *J*.

Sloane, Sloane.
I'm no one's clone.
That old rhyme?
You're making me groan.
I'm sweeter than
an ice-cream cone.
Strawberry,
chocolate chip,
cookie dough
Sloane.

Sloane, Sloane.
My name's well known.
I'm one of a kind,
a twin, not a clone.
When I rhyme
I'm in the zone.
I'm skinny-jean,
fashion-queen,
never-mean
Sloane.

December 11

TRY HARD

Rachel Chieko Stein

My mom says I should try hard,
get straight As.
"You're smart," she says.

My dad says I should try hard,
speak up more.
"You're too quiet," he says.

When I came
to Emerson Elementary
in kindergarten,

I tried hard
to get the best grades
and raise my hand.

But it was like the popular kids
overheard what my parents said.
So they called me "Try Hard."

At recess, I played with girls
who don't fit in, like Sydney and Katie,
my best school friends.

If our class gets split up, sent to new schools,
will the kids be nicer?
Probably not.

When you do all your homework,
ace every test,
and teachers always choose you,

someone is going to make fun of you,
no matter how hard
you try to fit in.

December 15
· · · · · · · · ·
CRACK THE WHIP
Sloane Costley

At recess we play Crack the Whip.
　　We hold hands, make a line.
　　　　Hannah,
　　　　　　Shoshanna, me,
　　　　　　　Brianna, Gaby,
　　　　　　　　　sometimes Rachel Stein.
　　　　　　　Jason, Ben, and
　　　　　　that new kid, Tyler,
　　　　　rush up and push
　　　　into the line.
　　(Ben always *happens*
to end up holding hands
with Rachel Stein.)
　　Hannah pulls us
　　　across the blacktop,
　　　　fast as a swirling wind.
　　　　　We snake around, our line makes a half circle.

　　　　　　Hannah turns.
　　　　　Whip!
The head of the line goes left　　back of the line snaps right.
　　　　　　　The last person can't hold on,
　　　　　　　　　goes flying off
　　　　　　　　　in another directio

One day Shoshanna
    stayed inside to help Ms. Hill,
        so I grabbed
            Hannah's hand,
                held on tight as I could.
                    We ran fast, faster.
                        When Shoshanna came out—
                                        back of the line for her.
                            We spun around
                        the basketball hoop.
                    Whip!

                                    Shoshanna
                                        flew away.

December 15

THE POETRY PROMPT JAR
Katie McCain

For Ms. Hill

I am stuck.
I cannot rhyme.
My words are weak
as tadpole slime.

I dip my hand
into the jar
of poem starts
from near and far.

There's tanka poems
from Japan,
Shakespearean sonnets
(I'm not a fan).

A limerick?
No. They're too rude.
Why not an ode
to my favorite food?

When writer's block
has made me pout,
the prompt jar's here
to help me out.

If you're going to be friends with Hannah Wiles,
better practice repeating "Me too."
Get used to wearing the clothes that she likes
and sticking to Hannah like glue.
She'll always ask your opinion on stuff
and pretend that she likes something new.
But if she says, "Do you like skiing?"
you should shrug and ask Hannah, "Do you?"

One day, we played Truth or Dare at lunch.
Hannah dared me to make Rachel cry.
She said it would be really easy
because Rachel is quiet and shy.
So I sat by Rachel at Hebrew School
and told her, "Your nose is so flat!
There isn't a Jewish girl I've ever seen
whose nose is so wide and so fat."
I know that Rachel Stein's mother
was born and grew up in Japan,
but I didn't know that I would cry, too.
That wasn't in Hannah's plan.

So when Hannah sat next to Norah Hassan
during gym class and gave me a wink,
and said Norah's head scarf looked like a dishrag,
and asked, "Shoshie, what do you think?"
I said, "I'm done being your friend, Hannah Wiles.
I'm done with saying 'Me too.'
Norah can cover her hair if she likes
without getting permission from you."
Now Norah and I sit together at lunch
and Hannah has somebody new
to like what she likes and dress in her style
and follow her saying "Me too."

"You can't be Jewish."
But I've never even
been to Japan.

December 19
• • • • • • • •
SNOW DAY
Tyler La Roche

Snowball fight at the Emerson playground!
Norah, Ben and Jason, Brianna and me.
Ow! It was cold. I've never touched real snow before.
Whoosh! Look out! Ben found a place to hide,
      under the slide.

Don't knock down our snowman. We spent
All day building him, me and my friends.
Yesterday, I finally felt like I belong here.

We have indoor recess.
It is too cold to go out.
Snow covers the ground.
Raj asks what I am writing.
He says, "Ugh! More poetry!"

December 23
• • • • • • • •
JERUSALEM
Norah Hassan

In Jerusalem my grandfather had a lemon tree.
Every day, we went to his house and picked lemons.
My sister squeezed them. I added sugar and soda water.
We said, "We are drinking sunshine."

In my new country, I see bare winter trees. No lemons.
Every day after school, my sister goes next door.
She watches our neighbor's baby.
Our apartment is so quiet, so small.
At school, I feel quiet and small.

But when Shoshanna sits with me at school,
I can't stop talking. She wants me to tell her
about Jerusalem and the lemon tree.
Shoshanna has invited me to her house
during winter break so I can teach her
how to make fizzy lemonade.

I hope our whole class goes to Montgomery Middle.
If we're sent to two different schools,
how will we stay friends?
I want to go back to Jerusalem one day,
and tell someone who never came to America
about my friend Shoshanna.

For Christmas
Grandpa gave me a photograph
of his great-grandfather
Benjamin Jones, infantry soldier
in the Civil War.
He stands for a portrait,
pistol in one hand,
Bible in the other.
Benjamin Jones looks tall
in his slouched cap
and dark jacket.
From a family of slaves
to fighting for our country.
His face looks scared and proud.
Grandpa knows that Rennie, George,
and Norah asked me
to help them write a petition,
so our whole class will sign up
to save Emerson Elementary.
But I didn't say yes
until Grandpa gave me the photograph
of my great-great-
great-grandfather
Benjamin Jones.

George Furst, Edgar Lee Jones, and Rennie Rawlins
Typed by Norah Hassan

We the People of Ms. Hill's Fifth Grade,
in Order to give a more perfect Understanding
of the importance of our student voices
here at Emerson Elementary,
seek to establish a Protest by our Classroom,
which hath Studied the U.S. Constitution and Civil Rights,
to Provide our United opinion
regarding the fate of our beloved Emerson Elementary,
and Demand that the Board of Education
promote general Knowledge about its plans,
and share the Blessings of Facts
with ourselves and all Emerson
and Montgomery Middle Students.
Thus we do create and Submit this Petition
to halt the razing of Our School
indefinitely.

Signed in Equality on this 6th Day of January

My
mom
is an
architect.
I asked her to speak
to the fifth grade on Career Day.
Oh, no! She brought drawings of the new supermarket.

Her
work
wants to
build the store.
She didn't tell me.
Some surprise! My class glared at me.
I couldn't even talk to her. My mom, the traitor.

(Thanks, Joni Mitchell!
Inspired by the song: "Big Yellow Taxi")

They're paving our school
to put up a grocery store
with a sushi bar, a valet,
and weird food like wild boar.

Don't it always seem to you
that the grown-ups never ask if we care?
They're gonna pave our school,
put up a grocery store.

They'll take all our desks,
put 'em in a huge landfill,
and they'll tax our parents,
'cause someone's gotta pay the bill.

Don't it always seem to you
that the grown-ups never ask if we care?
They're gonna pave our school,
put up a grocery store.

Hey, Katie's mom,
put away those supermarket plans now.
We'll keep our leaky roof,
but don't throw us out in the street,
please!

Don't it always seem to you
that the grown-ups never ask if we care?
They're gonna pave our school,
put up a grocery store.
They're gonna pave our school
and put up a grocery store.

January 9
• • • • • •
RUMORS
Brianna Holmes

Is it true?
Shoshanna's
ignoring
Hannah?

Is it true?
Rachel's
crushing
on Ben?

I heard
George's
parents
have split up

and
somebody
likes
Jason Chen.

I heard
that
Ms. Hill
is retiring.

I heard
Edgar's
granddad
is sick.

I heard
Katie's
mother
is hiring folks.

Is that true?
My mom
needs a job
quick!

January 12

HUNGRY YELLOW BULLDOZERS

Rennie Rawlins

I can picture them
sitting at the edge
of our kickball field.
Two yellow bulldozers
crouched outside,
ready to eat our school
in one greedy gulp.
I can picture them
staring at our
rickety old school,
ready to pounce.
They plan to tear up
the parking lot first,
rumbling closer and closer.
Then the basketball courts
will be gobbled up.
And when the old school
is abandoned . . . POUNCE.
Well, look out, bulldozers.
We are Ms. Hill's fifth grade,
and we've got plans for you.

All I did was ask
the kids in our class
to sign the petition.
I thought everyone would sign,
like a fifth-grade
Declaration of Independence.

But Katie said
could she please go last.
I guess she had to think about it,
whether it was worth
going against her mom.
"You don't have to sign it,"
I told Katie.

Bam! She slapped her desk.
"Give it here, George," she said.
"Just because my mom
wants to tear down this school
doesn't mean I automatically agree."

Then she signed the petition
in giant cursive letters.
I wasn't trying to make her mad!
I will never understand girls.

Dear Ms. Hill,

You are right.
We shouldn't blame Katie.
Her mother is doing her job,
and what she thinks
is right for her family.
A daughter should be loyal
to her mother.

As my father says,
we all have opinions,
but a family, like a school,
is not a democracy.
Children may speak,
but adults may choose
not to listen.

Pizza
Fried chicken
Snowballs
Slurpees

Taco truck
Donuts
Coffee
Chinese

With all this
great food
who needs
groceries?

January 16
• • • • • •
FOOD DESERT
Norah Hassan

When Ms. Hill says
this neighborhood
is a food desert,
at first I think, No.
I lived in a real desert.
We shopped every day
at the outdoor market.
Stalls filled with olives,
cucumbers, tomatoes.

Except, in this neighborhood,
we don't have a market.
When my parents work late
and there's no food in the house,
my sister and I can't walk
to a grocery store for fresh fruit.

The closest oasis in this desert
is the gas-station shop.
If we don't have much money
and it's cold outside,
that's where my sister and I
buy dinner.

When you're hungry
in the desert,
you'll eat anything.
Cacti, rattlesnake.
Even salty, swampy
ramen noodles
taste delicious.

January 20
· · · · · · · ·
WHAT'S FOR DINNER?
Brianna Holmes

When Ms. Hill tells us
about food deserts,
Norah and I look at each other.

I've seen Norah and her sister
at the gas-station store.
Fruits and vegetables?
Not unless you want to eat
beat-up brown bananas
and celery that looks like
it wants to flop over and die.

So . . . what are you going to buy?
Something frozen?
Something sweet?
The chicken's fried,
but at least it's meat.

Norah lives in my neighborhood.
We know all about food deserts.

In my food desert . . .

the sand is all brown sugar,
the sun looks like an egg,
the camels have spaghetti hair
to cover up their heads,
the cacti taste like gummy bears,
the candy rocks are free.
At lunchtime this food desert
is the place I want to be.

January 22
• • • • • • •
AFTER OUR CLASS DEBATE
Tyler La Roche

My mom and I just moved here,
so I didn't know there used to be
a supermarket in our neighborhood.
I didn't know there used to be
a cheese shop, a bakery,
and something Ms. Hill called
a fishmonger's. Instead we have
a karate dojo, a Chinese restaurant,
and a bunch of empty stores.
I didn't know this school
used to have so many kids
they needed portable classrooms
in the back to fit them all.

My mom and I just moved here,
but I already know
every morning when I walk
into Emerson Elementary,
all the teachers call, "Good morning."
My friends shout, "Hi, Ty!"
like it's the funniest thing
they ever said. I already know
why people like this school,
why they want to stay
for middle school.

My mom and I just moved here,
so it's easy for me to see both sides.

I don't want to
think about the reasons why
tearing down our school
might be a good thing.

Brianna says her mom is looking for a job.
Norah needs a grocery store she can walk to.
Katie's mom told our class that the supermarket
will bring more families to our neighborhood.

I don't want to
think about the reasons why
tearing down our school
might be a good thing.

My mom says when one chapter ends
another one is beginning.
I don't want to think about
what might happen if I turn the page.

THIRD QUARTER
• • • • • • • • • • • •

WHEN YOUR SCHOOL HAS OLD WINDOWS
Katie McCain

New seats again.
Now I sit next to Ben.
The window's nearby.
I can see the blue sky.
The sun's on my face.
I imagine a place,
stretching out on the sand
in my bathing suit and
suddenly—*BRRR!*
The cold temperature
is like an ice bath
in the middle of math.
The sun had me baking.
Now I shiver. I'm shaking.
There's a draft in this spot.
Ms. Hill, I cannot
sit here in this breeze.
I am going to . . .
                    ACHOO!

I WANTED TO STAY HOME FROM SCHOOL TODAY
Edgar Lee Jones

I wanted to stay home from school today.
My grandpa didn't get out of bed
to get the newspaper.

I wanted to stay home from school today.
Mom called the ambulance because
Grandpa's left side was acting frozen.

I wanted to stay home from school today.
He couldn't talk or walk,
couldn't say, "Learn something today, Eddie."

I wanted to stay home from school today.
My head's filled up with Grandpa.
I'm at my desk, but I'm not here.

Sloane brought home our invitation
to Hannah Wiles's birthday party.
Hannah's father is getting a giant truck
covered inside and out with flat-screen TVs,
so we can play every video game ever created.
When the truck drives up to Hannah's house,
most of our class will be there,
playing,
     laughing
         together.

Sloane said I'd better not embarrass her
or hang out with anyone uncool.
Maybe I won't go to the party.
When Sloane spends time
with Hannah Wiles
she acts like she doesn't
even
    want to
        know me.

My dad was flipping through the paper
the way he does every morning,
quizzing me and my stepmom
on current events and stuff
he thinks we should know.

"Listen to this letter to the editor,"
he said, shaking his head the way he does
when I'm not being patient enough
with my (half) brothers.

*"'If you walk through Emerson Elementary,
you will see and feel the difference
a school can make in the lives of its students.
You will see how a strong community
builds character.'"*

Dad said schools need to do more
than build character. He said
you can't measure character.
The person who wrote the letter
didn't say a word about academics
or standardized test scores,
and test scores at Emerson, Dad said,
are pitiful.

"What's character?" I asked.
He said, "My point exactly,"
and started talking about
low enrollment and the money
the school system will make
when it sells the prime real estate
underneath our pitiful school.

January 30
. . . .
FACES
Norah Hassan

The hallways of Emerson are filled with families
on International Night. Tonight, our school
reminds me of shopping in the Old Jerusalem market.
I remember when I was small,
going to the pepper stand with Jaddi.
Fifty types of peppers to eat!
Pale green, yellow as a lemon, dark brown, red,
each with a different flavor.
On International Night,
the halls are as noisy as an outdoor market.
Children shout. Parents call, "Let's go!"
in so many languages.
In English, the teachers say, "See you tomorrow!"
I find an empty doorway where I can stand still.
I watch. I listen.
If they take away our school
and build a supermarket with a thousand shelves,
there will be no empty doorway
for a girl like me to watch the passing faces.
If they take away our school,
where will the voices of our families
meet to say, "Hello, neighbor! Hello!"

It's weird to see your teacher
doing normal things
like shopping for valentines
(were those for our class?)
in a non-school place like Target,
but I'm glad you finally
got to meet my dad, Ms. Hill.
He thinks you're smart. I could tell
by all the questions he asked
about when you were in college
and you marched in protests.
(I told him about the picture
of you on Capitol Hill.)
He shook your hand and thanked you
because you encouraged me
to get involved with the political process.
Whatever that means.
I guess it's true, you motivated me
to take action, even though those sit-ins
you were telling my dad about
don't sound very active to me.

Señorita Hill,

Gracias.
Esta es la primera vez
que hemos tenido un intérprete
para la conferencia
de padres y maestros
desde que llegamos aquí.
Mi mamá estaba tan contenta.
A ella le gustó la señora May.
Yo también me alegré.
Mis hermanas
no tuvieron que venir a la escuela
a traducirle a nuestra madre.
Eso es bueno.
Ellas no tienen que saber
que soy buena en matemáticas
pero todavía mala
para escribir
en inglés.

Gracias, Gaby

Dear Miss Hill,

Thank you.
This is the first time
that we had an interpreter
for the conference
of parents and teachers
since we come to this country.
My mother was very happy.
She liked Señora May.
I also feel happy.
My sisters
do not have to come to the school
to translate for our mother.
This is good.
They do not have to know
that I do well in math
but I am still bad
when I write
in English.

Gracias, Gaby

When my brother and me
get all As and Bs,
my mom takes us out for fondue.
Fruit, brownies, and cake,
all dipped in a lake
of chocolate-marshmallow goo.
We have so much fun,
but when the bill comes
I see that look on my mom's face.
Our money's real tight.
I wish that tonight
we'd eaten dessert at our place.

Mark and me, we were the only boys
who tried out for the spring musical,
Beauty and the Beast.
Our chorus teacher is the director.
He said I have the best *"bonjour"* of anybody.
My mom got a good laugh about that
'cause my family is Cajun.
We came up north from Texas.
Mom got tired of all those hurricanes
screaming down our town,
tearing shingles off our roof
and flooding the house.
Mom found another university to teach at.
It's a good job, but sometimes she tells me
she's homesick. She's kind of like Belle,
doesn't know anyone in the castle,
and making friends is hard.
At least Belle had all that singing silverware.
And me, I've got Mark. We figure
our teacher's got to choose
one of us for Gaston
and the other one for the Beast.
So I'm in, piece of cake.
All I had to do was show up
and try out.

February 9
• • • • • • • •
TALENT
Mark Fernandez

If it wasn't for Gaby,
I would have never
gotten up onstage
and played my guitar
in the talent show.
Sure, I'm in a band,
but when Zoo Creatures
performs, we wear
those funny animal masks.
With a mask on,
I don't get as nervous.
Gaby helped me,
so I'm returning the favor,
bringing her and Tyler with me
to try out for the school musical.
Her English still isn't the best,
but Gaby can sing.
She's got enough talent
to fill the whole stage.

When it's time for recess,
we rush outside with a whoosh,
like a stormy wind.
I grab a basketball before they're all taken,
pass it across the blacktop to Rachel.
But lately she doesn't want to shoot hoops
with me.

Hannah's teaching all the girls
cheerleading.
Ugh. If Rachel wants to clap her hands
and copy Hannah's dance moves
because she hopes
a certain boy is watching,
I've got no time for her.
I told her so.

And Rachel said, "Fine."

I went to sit
by the brick wall behind school,
where Ben and I
used to hunt for frogs.

Sloane left cheerleading to find me.
We sat leaning against the brick wall
for the rest of recess.
Sloane didn't even care
that we were sitting on dirt
and she was wearing her new jeans.
We talked about friends and crushes
and how everything is changing
except for my
number one best friend forever,
sister Sloane.

Oh, how I long
for the most relaxing
school day of the year.
On Pajama Day
my mom doesn't attack
my bed head with a brush.
My backpack is stuffed
with pillows instead of books.
I slide down the hall
like a penguin skidding on ice,
because giant fuzzy slippers
and floor wax are a great combination.
This morning Ms. Hill asked us
to take out our pillows
and write poems on the floor.
(Everyone laughed
when Mark started to snore.)
I wore rainbow frog pajamas,
which unfortunately meant
Newt followed me around
until Jason took him
to borrow Connect Four
from the fourth grade.
I love Pajama Day.

```
                    BLACK
                   ORIOLES
                BASEBALL CAP
                  FACEFACE
                  FACEFACE
                  FACEFACE
                    FACE
                    NECK
             SHIRTSHIRTSHIRT
          SHIRTSHIRTSHIRTSHIRT
          SHIRT SHIRTSK ATSHIRT
         SHIRT  SHIRTSTIET SHIRT
         ARM SHIRTSHMT ARM
         ARM SHIRTSHIRT ARM
         ARM SHIRTSHIRT ARM
         ARM SHIRTSHIRT ARM
         ARM SHIRTSHIRT ARM
         ARM SHIRTSHIRT ARM
         ARM JEANSJEANS ARM
         ARM JEANSJEANS ARM
       HAND JEANSJEANS HAND
       HAND JEANS JEANS HAND
            JEANS JEANS
            JEANS JEANS
            JEANS JEANS
          J    NS JE    S
            JEANS JEANS
            JEANS JEANS
            JEANS JEANS
            JEANS JEANS
         COOLVANS VANSCOOL
         COOLVANS VANSCOOL
```

Valentine
pink, frilly card
opening, reading, smiling
hearts, love, hugs, friendship
embarrassing, sweet note
from my BFF
Sydney

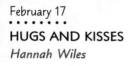

HUGS AND KISSES
Hannah Wiles

Before she left, my mom gave me
a glass jar filled
with chocolate Hugs and Kisses.
She said whenever I need a hug
or a kiss goodnight,
even though she is far away,
I can take one out of the jar.
Yesterday
when I got home from school
there were silver wrappers
all over my bed, on the floor.
My stepmom, Heather, was mad . . .
at me!
         All that sugar
made my (half) brothers crazy.
They didn't take their naps.
That's how come
I wrote this extra poem.
Because I spent a lot of time
alone in my room. I finally get why
people want to save Emerson.
Losing our school is like
losing home, the place

where everyone understands you.
When my dad came upstairs
to get me for dinner, he said sorry
for what the boys did. He said
he'd buy me more chocolate.
But it won't be the same because
they won't be my mom's
hugs and kisses,
and this will never feel like home.

I had it all planned,
how I'd call my dad
and tell him Mrs. Stiffler
was sending our petition
to the Board of Education
and how Dad gave me the idea!
Then I'd ask him to come home
and help me write my speech
to the Board and the superintendent
of schools.

But that's not what happened.
Mrs. Stiffler called us down today.
She told Rennie, Norah,
Edgar, and me how proud she was
of our initiative. But she sighed
and said there is nothing
one principal and a group of fifth graders
can do to change the mind
of the mighty, all-powerful
Board of Education.

I faked it, acted like I was okay.
Don't worry, I told Rennie,
Norah, and Edgar in the hall.
We'll think of something.
We've been working all year
to save our school.
I can't let my friends
think it's over.
I can't tell my dad
our petition failed.

February 19
· · · · · · ·
IN THE PRINCIPAL'S OFFICE
Rennie Rawlins

Tip tap tip tap, the secretary's fingers
sound like rain on her keyboard.
We walk to Mrs. Stiffler's office,
me, George, Edgar, and Norah.
Boom baboom goes my heart,
heavy as a thunderstorm.
"What's this about?" Mrs. Stiffler sniffs.
Her nose is turning purple,
but her voice stays calm.
She slides our petition across her desk.

My voice shakes worse than a scared rabbit
when I tell her our class
is learning U.S. history
and part of that history
is standing up for our rights.
Mrs. Stiffler's office is quiet as a cloud,
but when she says no,
she won't send our petition to the Board,
it's a lightning bolt. The skies darken.
The downpour begins.

Edgar, Norah, and I shuffle down the hall.
No one wants to hear George's pep talk.
The whole class rushes up
when we walk in the door.
Our stormy faces give us away.
Ms. Hill says she's sorry.
The girls hug me. The boys say,
"Hey, you tried," but all I can think is . . .
what am I going to tell Phoenix?

The bad news is, our petition failed.
The Board won't ever know
some fifth graders wanted to save Emerson.

The worse news is
my grandpa is still in the hospital.
Sometimes he doesn't
recognize me.
I wish I could write a petition
to the doctors, or to God,
to make him better.

I wish I could talk to Grandpa
about the bad news.

I love sweeping the soft hairs of the brush across my palm.
I love rolling the brush in ink and water.
I love watching our art teacher's hands,
      teaching us to hold the brush right.
I love how Mr. Musay calls the hand position Tiger Mouth.
I love the dragonfly appearing on my paper.

I hate hearing from the next table, "Duh,
      of course she's good at Japanese painting."
I hate the hard words Sloane says, pretending to be nice.
      "I love your painting, Rachel."
I hate when she bumps my elbow and spills my ink.
I hate how she acts as if she's sorry.

I love how Mr. Musay swirls the ink blot into a water lily.
I love how he shows my painting to the whole class.

February 24

• • • • • • •

TISSUES

Sydney Costley

I have never seen
Rachel cry
before today.
I have seen her trip
over a jump rope
and skin her knee
on the blacktop
and say, "I'm fine."
I have seen her
not getting picked
for a part in the play
and pretend
to shrug it off.
But before today
I never saw
anyone
make her cry.
Good thing
I was there
to hand her tissues
under our desks.
She squeezed my hand.
Then she smiled
a little, back to being
my Rachel.

For S.B.

Remember second grade?
Our class had a stuffed dog
named Spike.
Everyone took turns
bringing Spike home.
We wrote down
all the things Spike did
in a blue notebook.
When my turn was over,
Spike went home with you
for the whole weekend.
I was so sad!
I didn't want to give up Spike.
I was crying in the book closet
when you came in
and asked me what was wrong.
You rubbed my back
and said, "Don't be sad, Hannah."
And you asked your mom
if I could sleep over
so I could spend one more day
with Spike. Before that day,
I'd never really noticed you.
Afterward, I thought we'd stay
best friends forever.

1) At the beginning of fifth grade
we played Four Square at recess every day.
Hannah was always QUEEN,
bouncing the ball and hitting it to me.
I stood in the PRINCESS square
just like in school, next to Hannah
because we were best friends.
I bounced and hit the ball
to Sloane, who always played MAID.

2) Hannah is like a rubber ball,
bouncing from one girl to the next.
Gentle one minute, then hitting hard
at Brianna in the DUNGEON.
Hannah always made Brianna miss
so she'd stay in the last spot.
Then one day Hannah hit the ball hard at me.
I missed. I had to stand in the dungeon.
I was so mad.

3) So I quit the game. For a week,
I stayed inside at recess, helping Ms. Hill.
But fifth grade is a lot like Four Square.
If you wait long enough
you move through the squares,
even when it feels like
you'll be in the dungeon forever.
Now I play with Norah,
Rennie, and Rachel.

4) We make up funny stuff.
"Lunch Tray" Four Square
is Baby Carrots, Applesauce,
Sloppy Joes, and Chocolate Milk.
No one feels bad about
being in the Chocolate Milk square.
I'm back in the game.
Four Square is fun
when no one's in the dungeon.

February 27
· · · · · · · ·
GIRL TALK
Sydney Costley

I asked my mother why
all the fifth-grade girls
had to stay in Ms. Hill's room
while the boys in our class
went to Mr. Musay's art room
to talk about bodies and stuff,
because that's really private.
My mom said some parents
don't talk to their kids
about that kind of thing, so
everyone has to learn it at school.
She said she would always
answer my questions
and I should never
feel ashamed.

I don't even know
what my questions are.
But I know
I'm not like the girls
who crack up every time
Ms. Hill says "puberty."
I wasn't the one
who started throwing
samples of feminine products
across the room.
It looked like a snowball fight.
A dozen maxi pads
flying over our heads.

I'd rather dissect owl pellets,
bird vomit filled with bones.
I'd rather Mrs. Stiffler
called my mother on the phone.
I'd rather hit my head in gym
so I'd get a concussion.
Anything to get me out
of this Disgusting Discussion.

ODE TO RECESS
Ben Kidwell

Twenty minutes of air.
Twenty minutes of dirt.
Twenty minutes of sky.
Twenty minutes to play.
Twenty minutes without any pink notes
   asking which girl I like.
Twenty minutes with no chairs, no pencils, no tests
   with round bubbles to fill in.
Twenty minutes till the recess monitor blows her whistle.
Twenty minutes of wondering whether the tall trees
   behind our school will get cut down in June.
Twenty minutes outside.
Twenty minutes of almost-freedom.

I brought a jar of tadpoles.
I caught them in the pond
behind my house.

They are moving,
wriggling black dots
in the water.

Half the girls said, "Ew!"
but Newt kept staring
at the tadpoles.

He asked me to be partners
for the science fair.
It's better than working alone.

Every Saturday, I grab my net,
run outside, meet Newt
at the frog pond.

We catch tadpoles,
take pictures to record
how much they've changed.

Every week, their tails are shorter,
stumps on their sides
transform into legs.

Every Saturday,
I say *Wow.* Who knew
Newt was so much fun?

March 5

CARDINAL WATCH
Norah Hassan

This winter was so gray
until I saw a flash of red
in the trees behind our apartment building—
a cardinal. Spring is near.
I put birdseed on my windowsill.
One morning when I woke up
he was there. So close!
My father said if I left more seeds
the cardinal would bring his wife.

She has dull feathers but a pretty beak.
It's almost pink. I drew pictures of them
in my science project journal.
My father says they are building a nest
in the woods between our apartment building
and Emerson's soccer field.
They use twigs, leaves, grass, and hair.
Each night, I take a few strands of hair
from my brush and leave them with the seeds.
My sister thinks this is disgusting,
but I think my hair will make the nest as strong
as a hudhud's nest in Jaddi's lemon tree.
The mother cardinal will weave my hair
into her little bowl of twigs
to keep the eggs protected from wind.
I hope the nest stays safe all spring,
even if the builders clear some trees
to make space for the new supermarket.

I see a pond in my neighborhood.
I hear northern spring peepers
calling to female frogs.
Whoosh! Raj's net splashes into water.
I feel something slimy in the net.
A tan frog squirms in my palm.
Hyla crucifer is the scientific name
for the frogs we are tracking.
They are the size of my thumbnail.
They are louder than my baby sister.
Raj is my science partner now.
I taste the juice my mom packed for us.
I smell the buttered popcorn
Raj brought to share. *Crunch!*

March 9
• • • • • •
HAMMY POWER!
Jason Chen

My hamster's name is Refried Beans.
He poops a lot when he eats greens.
His favorite things are his hamster wheel,
carrots, nuts, and an apple peel.
How much energy does he cause
running fast on tiny paws?
Dad hooked the wheel to an amp meter.
I took readings, 'cause I'm no cheater.
I spent three hours on calculations,
wrote the report, and took notations.
Even if he runs all night,
one hamster can't turn on a light.
And it would take a trillion hammies
to fuel a car down to Miami.
I like doing science at school.
(Katie said my project was cool.)

Why does he loan me his favorite books?
Why does he give me those puppy-dog looks?
Why won't he pass me when we run the mile?
Why does he have such a sweet, goofy smile?
Why does he like me? I can't work it out.
I'm crazy. I'm messy. I'm weird and I shout.
My toenails are silver. I dyed my hair blue.
I wrote "Hamster Hater" on top of my shoe.
Was it something I said? What could it be?
Out of all the fifth graders, why does he like me?

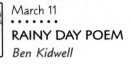

drip drip drip
Teacher. Hey, Teacher!
drip drip tap
Roof's leaking again.
drip tap tap
My desk needs a bucket
tap tap tap
whenever it rains.
tap tap splash
The rain is a drummer.
tap splash splash
It beats out a tune
splash splash splash
that gets louder and louder
splash splash flash
and ends with
kaBOOM!

Yesterday at recess,
Ben said
he wanted to show me
and Newt something
on the soccer field.
It was a tire mark
with treads deep enough
to hold a puddle.
In the water, we saw
squirming tadpoles.
Newt and I held some
cupped in our hands.
How will the tadpoles
grow into frogs
if this field
is a parking lot?

March 13
· · · · · · ·
TURTLE
Edgar Lee Jones

Made from walnut shell
Green felt for feet, head, tail
Sitting in my hand
I put it on the table
By his bed

Right now
in Ms. Hill's fifth grade,
eighteen students
are quietly
writing poems.

Right now
members of
the Board of Education
are touring
Emerson Elementary.
They're getting closer
to our classroom.

This morning
someone covered
the fifth-grade hall
with posters.
Right now,
everywhere I look,
I see three small words,
Save Our School.
Three big letters,
SOS.

Right now,
I'm wondering . . .
will Mrs. Stiffler
be proud
of our initiative?

No one knows
   who put up all those posters before school this morning.
No one knows
   who had a poster party at their house last night.
No one knows
   who was invited.
No one knows
   where all the paints, markers, and poster board came from.
No one knows
   who figured out the Board of Ed was visiting Emerson today.
No one knows
   who thought of doing a poster protest.

No one wants
   Mrs. Stiffler to blame you, Ms. Hill,
so it's better if you don't know.

So it's lunchtime
and I'm eating with Hannah Wiles,
who happens to be my new best friend,
when the principal does her fast walk
into the cafeteria.
Her nose is all purple
(it does that when she's mad).
She clears her throat (gross),
and I can tell she's trying
not to yell about the posters
and how we defaced school property
when Very Special Guests
were touring the building.
Blah blah blah.
But then Mrs. Stiffler
says something about
taking away
our Moving Up ceremony.
Hannah and I stare at each other
with our mouths wide open in shock.
Can a principal do that?

Ms. Hill picked me for Captain of Patrols.
I wear a badge and help kids cross the street.
It's like I'm older brother to the world
when I tell students, "Hey! Slow down those feet."

I'm always quiet when I ride the bus.
I get straight As. My homework's never late.
But I got mad when Stiffler yelled at us
and told us that we might not graduate.

She left the room. Somebody threw their snack.
At first I ducked when food began to fly.
But then I thought, *Why not?* and with a crack
I popped my bag of chips into the sky.

I laughed inside when people said, "How cool!
I never thought that Raj would break a rule."

Our class was bad.
We broke the rules.
Everyone threw food.
It was loud.
After lunch, Mrs. Stiffler came to fifth grade.
I didn't like it when she yelled.
And then Ms. Hill said
we know better ways
to solve our problems. She said
she was disappointed in our class.
I got upset.
I left my seat without permission.
I went to the cafeteria.
Mr. Dutcher is the janitor.
I helped him clean up.
I swept the mess with his extra broom.
I heard him tell my aide, Mr. Ron White,
"Nothing wrong with this kid."
I want to save our school
so I can always visit Mr. Dutcher.

My father made me brownies
to celebrate
the fact that I marched
into Mrs. Stiffler's office
     (I told him
     I wasn't marching,
     but he said permit him
     to embellish),
burst through the door
after the fifth-grade
food fight,
and said
     (actually,
     asserted,
     according to
     my father)
that the fifth grade
would not have to protest
if she actually
listened to us.

(That's when Mrs. Stiffler
called Mom's work
complaining about
a fifth-grade mutiny.)
I got my first
detention ever
for being
"insubordinate."
      (I looked it up.
      In means "not."
      Subordinate means
      "inferior.")
I like the way
that sounds.

24 Marzo
• • • • • • •
HACIENDO EL PAPEL DE LA BELLA
Gaby Vargas

En casa, me miro en el espejo.
Mi hermana golpea la puerta del baño.
Piensa que me estoy peinando
pero estoy ensayando para la pieza de teatro.

Recito mi parte
en la escena donde la Bestia se muere.
Miro en el espejo.
Pienso en Mark con maquillaje
y una peluca muy peluda. Debo decir
"Te amo, Bestia!"
Mark siempre se ríe
cuando la practicamos.

Por mucho tiempo yo hacía
como si sintiera algo especial por Mark.
Pero quizás fue sólo un medio-amorcito.
Quizás yo y Mark sólo somos buenos amigos.

In my house, I see myself in the mirror.
My sister hits the door of the bathroom.
She thinks that I am combing my hair,
but I am practicing for the play.

I recite my part
in the scene where Beast dies.
I look in the mirror.
I think of Mark with makeup
and a very hairy wig. I have to say,
"I love you, Beast!"
Mark always laughs
when we practice this part.

For much time I was thinking
that I feel something special for Mark.
But perhaps it was a half love.
Maybe me and Mark are only good friends.

BEING THE BEAST
Mark Fernandez

I put on a hairy mask.
You can still see a little skin around my eyes
so Sloane's mother covers it
with brown makeup.
I have whiskers and furry gloves with claws.
It doesn't look like me at all.
I am the Beast.

This whole school year
I've been acting like someone else.
Pretending to be funny
so no one would feel sorry for me.
My friends Tyler and Gaby
don't mind when I'm sad.
And Jason draws those flip books
to make me laugh.
Laughing feels strange.
Bad and good.

Before the last song of the show
I have to run backstage,
take off the mask and the hairy gloves.
Sloane's mom brushes my hair,
wipes the makeup off my face.
I let out a big breath.
That costume is hot!
It feels good to see my curly hair
and a human nose.
I feel like myself
for the first time
since my father died.
Sloane's mother calls it
my transformation
from Beast to boy.

Dear Ms. Hill,

I am sorry I put on Mark's Beast costume,
jumped out of the coat closet,
and started singing at you
in the middle of quiet reading time yesterday.
I thought you were going to be someone else.
I'm sorry you didn't think it was funny.
Mrs. Stiffler is already mad
at the whole fifth grade for interfering
with plans to close this school.
Please don't send me to her office.

This is not my best poem of the year.
I'll put a good rhyme at the end.
I hope my joke did not offend.

My sisters spent a whole bunch
of their babysitting money
so I'd have the most Stargrams
of anyone in the cast.

When the show was over
and we were done taking bows,
I went into the hall and saw
the walls covered in paper stars.

Twinkling, yellow. I read them all.
"Hey, Mark. Way to go, bro!"
"You may be the Beast
but you sing like an angel."

My sisters thought
I was embarrassed. They didn't know
about me and our Papi
looking at *las estrellas*.

FOURTH QUARTER
· · · · · · · · · · · · · ·

I hear my mother chattering Arabic into her cell phone.
I smell the jet engines when we arrive at the airport in DC.
I see my grandfather! Jaddi looks tired, carrying his luggage,
but I feel him squeeze me tight and shake from laughing.
This is what happiness tastes like.

MARVELOUS MATZO
Rachel Chieko Stein

Passover is my favorite holiday.
I love matzo for lunch, spread thick
with cream cheese and strawberry jam.
I love how the matzo crunches
around the soft cream cheese
and gooey jelly.

I promised my dad I would eat
at the allergy-free table during Passover
even though people eat bread there,
because the janitors
keep that table really clean.
But when I sit at the allergy-free table,
my friends think I am mad at them.

"Why aren't you sitting with us?"
"Why do Jewish people eat weird food?"
"You have to eat that for a whole week?"
"Don't you miss bread?"

I told my dad I wanted a thermos of soup
instead of a delicious matzo, cream cheese,
and jam sandwich for lunch.
He took out a recipe
covered with chocolate streaks.
"Aunt Jennie's Matzo Candy."
We buttered matzos, baked them
until they were hot, spread them
with chocolate and butterscotch chips.

Melting, crispy, buttery, sweet. Mmmm.
Dad said, "I think this is the right medicine.
See the bottom of Aunt Jennie's recipe?
To stop teasing, administer
one dose to classmates."
I didn't see anything written on the recipe.
But when I shared Aunt Jennie's candy at lunch,
no one said matzo was weird.

April 9
· · · · ·
YOU'VE GOT A FRIEND
Tyler La Roche

I liked the song
we listened to this morning.
Music always gives my day
a dose of sunshine
(as my mom likes to say).

That song was the helping hand
our class needed
to get us smiling again.
It's good to know
we've got a friend-
ly teacher.

My sister says sixth grade is
    no parents at the bus stop, new friends,
    drama in the hallways, tears and shouting,
    laughing so loud everyone in the lunchroom stares,
    elementary school friends acting like they don't know you.
My sister says sixth grade is
    crushes shorter than a phone call,
    texting under your desk and having to pay your own bill,
    Friday night dances in the gym
    feeling awkward dancing with friends,
    maybe even boys—so what if they're shorter than you—
    tons of homework, even on weekends.
My sister says sixth grade is
    kissing in the empty band room,
    seeing the whole thing posted online,
    hoping your mom doesn't find out.
My sister says sixth grade is
    hard sometimes
    in the middle of the day
    when you just need someone
    who loves you.
"But I'll be there," my sister says.
    She promises, no matter where we end up,
    she'll say hi in the hallway,
    and if I get sad, I can find her.
    Sixth grade is everything changing
    except my older sister.

April 13
• • • • •
LITTLE RIVER
Rajesh Rao

Some of us
went on a trip
to Little River Middle.
The halls
of that school
made me feel like a frog
in an overcrowded pond.
Teachers don't
line kids up
and walk them quietly
from here to there.
Instead
kids jostle, push,
yell, and rush
across the halls
to class. Wow!
I can see my future.
Little River Middle is
no teachers
treating us like babies,
no younger sisters
for me to watch over.
FINALLY
freedom.

Holy Angels School—
I love that name.
Sloane and Brianna
think the blue dresses
Holy Angels girls wear
are dorky. Gaby can't believe
I'm going to a school
where there are no boys.
But I told them
if your mom was in the army,
and she was stationed
in a place whose name
you can barely pronounce,
you would want
to go to Holy Angels.
You would wear
a plain blue dress
and go to religion class,
and you would not miss boys
one bit.

I unwrap one chocolate kiss
and say a prayer for my mother
every morning, every night,
that she is safe,
that she's all right.
I think the angels
will listen harder
to my prayers
when I am at Holy Angels.
I hope they can hear me.

Ms. Hill,
I don't think our class
understands
the First Amendment.
Most of them never
lived without
freedom of speech,
but I have.

I don't think our class
understands
that someone can
get in trouble
for saying what they think,
or lose their job
for speaking
against their boss.

I don't think our class
understands
why we spent
our social studies period
learning about
First Amendment rights
and how people staged sit-ins
during the civil rights
movement.

But I understand why,
when we packed up today,
you told our class
there is a Board meeting
coming up soon
and it is open
to the public.

Student council means nothing
If the elected students aren't given the chance
To make their voices heard.

If we are determined to save our school,
No one has the right to ignore us.

ODE TO MY MOM
Rennie Rawlins

My mom may look little,
but she is the mighty
Angela P. Rawlins, Esquire.
That means she's a lawyer.
She does mom stuff, too,
makes the best
double chocolate chip cookies
in the universe, reads books
with me and Phoenix every night.
But if my mom thinks
you've done someone wrong ...
look out.
I told her how Mrs. Stiffler
said she would cancel
the fifth-grade celebration.
My mom's eyes got as sharp
and dark as pencil tips.
She said, "We will see about that."
Between the two of us,
I swear we called every single family
with a student at our school.
George and Norah are worried
no one's going to show up
at the Board of Ed meeting.
They are underestimating
Angela P. Rawlins, Esquire,
and me.

Ms. Hill, I have a secret.
I don't want to go to Montgomery Middle.
Crossing a hallway between schools
isn't going to change anything,
no matter how much the teachers clap for us.
We'll still be with the same kids as always.
The problem with K–8 is,
I can't take three more years
of them calling me Sydney Kidney.
The problem with K–8 is,
Brianna told everyone
I'm the tomboy twin, and now
that's who the whole fifth grade
expects me to be.
If the Board of Ed sells this place,
all the students will be split up.
That's why I'm not going
to the sit-in at the Board.
I want a middle school
where no one knows who I am,
a place where I can decide for myself
how I should dress,
which kids I'm crushing on,
a place where I can figure out
who I want to be,
but please keep that a secret.

April 21
• • • • • •
STAND UP, SIT DOWN
Hannah Wiles

The phone rings.
I can hardly believe what I see.
Shoshanna's number on the ID.
She says George is planning a protest
for our school to stay open.
She wants me to come.
Her dad will drive us.
What should I do?
I ask my stepmom, Heather. She says
why is Shoshanna being nice to me
all of a sudden?
I ask my dad. He says,
"Good riddance. Emerson
should have shut down years ago."
Then I email my mom. She writes
back to say I should stand up
for what I want.
So I call Shoshanna.
I will ride with her to the meeting.
I will sit down
with the rest of my class.

Hello, my name
is George Washington Furst.
I am a student
at Emerson Elementary School
and president
of our school's
student council.
Students, parents, and teachers
from Emerson Elementary
and Montgomery Middle
are here tonight
to give
the Board of Education
a petition
with over five hundred
signatures.
We are asking
the Board
to delay its plans
to close our school
in June.

Some of my classmates
and other students
have prepared statements
explaining why
the Board
should save our school.
We plan
to sit in this room
until you hear
all
of our voices.

How many hours do we have to sit here
before we are called to the stand?
How many kids must fill up the Board room
before we can speak as we planned?
And how many times will we sing this old song
before Ms. Hill's students get banned?
The answer, my friend, is ...
     A lot of hours.
     A lot of kids.
     A lot of times.

I'm glad you taught us those old songs, Ms. Hill,
so we had something to do while we waited
for the Board to let us speak.
Answers blowing in the wind
can get pretty loud
when you're trying to make grown-ups
pay attention.

ODE TO MY GUITAR
Mark Fernandez

You were a gift
from my father
on my ninth birthday.
I strum you
and I hear
Papi's voice
teaching me the chords.
I remember his hands
placing my fingers
on the frets.
I hold you close,
my old guitar,
and you
play happy music.
I bring you
wherever I go,
as if you were
my best friend.
We played together
when my class
sang songs of protest
at the Board
of Education.
Papi
would be proud of us.

I pushed my way through the crowd.
I walked right past my mother
and her fancy architectural drawings
of the new supermarket.

My mom gave me a thumbs-up.
She was the one who told me
    how to dress
    what to say
so the Board would take me seriously.

I stood in front
of the Board of Education
and told them how,
even though our neighborhood
needs a supermarket,
we wouldn't be a neighborhood
without our school.

Mom said she's impressed with me,
even though we disagree.

April 28
• • • • • •
BORED AT THE BOARD
Jason Chen

There was a bored student named Chen
who'd been sitting for hours, but then
he said, "Why should I wait?
I'll ask Kate on a date."
She said yes! Let's give Chen an "Amen!"

My father promised he'd come
to the Board of Ed meeting to hear my speech.
But he didn't.

Since my dad wasn't there,
I couldn't show him how hard I worked
to keep our school the way it's always been.

I won't get another chance to tell the Board
they should talk to the students
before they decide to close our school.

Just like my dad
should have talked to me and Mom
before he left our family.

WHAT I MISSED
Edgar Lee Jones

I missed the sit-in at the Board.
I missed the waiting, being ignored.
I missed it when we lost our fight,
and Emerson was sold that night.
I missed it all. I wasn't there.
I spent all night in a hospital chair
visiting Grandpa with my dad.
I miss his smile. He looks real bad.

I know what I'm going to buy
with my Easter money from Grandmom.
I've got my heart set on a red velvet bag
filled with Tiger's Eye stones.

One stone is for Phoenix
so she'll feel strong as a tiger
at her new school next year.

One stone is for my friend Norah
so she won't forget me when
we go to different middle schools.

One stone is for Edgar
to give his grandpa, because
Tiger's Eye brings good luck.

I'll keep one stone for myself
so I always remember
I can roar like a tiger.

But the biggest stone,
I'm saving that one
for George.

He's the spark
that lit up our class this year.
He's the glint of fire
in the Tiger's Eye.

May 5
• • • • •
MAKEOVER
Sydney Costley

Mom said I could change my look
over the summer
before middle school starts.
I asked, "Why wait?"
Norah already looks different,
mysterious and older
since she started wearing
her hijab every day.
I think it would be cool
to look older,
but not by covering myself up.
Over spring break
Mom took me to her salon,
dyed my hair black
with a pink streak in front,
gave me a short pixie cut.
She says it shows off my face.
I feel light
without all of that long hair.
At school, everyone says,
"Sydney, is that you?
You look so different."
I like it. I was always
different from Sloane
on the inside.
We are still twins,
even though
I have been made over.

When it's almost summer
and the sun stays out late,
my favorite place is the park.
The younger kids are leaving
because it's their bedtime.
My brother and I
have the whole place to roam,
me on my bike, him on his scooter.
We ride past the big tree
humming with insects.
The breeze on my face could be
air moved by a thousand cicada wings.
Our wheels rumble like thunder
over the wooden bridge.
We find the baseball diamond—
empty!—so we skid over the bases,
kicking up orange dust.
I forget about torn-down schools
and friends who are changing.
I forget about homework
and teachers who shouldn't retire.
Then we roll along the shadowy path
toward home, my brother and me,
in the deepening dark
of an almost-summer night.

Jaddi is going home soon,
back to Jerusalem.

He asked me to fly back with him,
spend the summer at his house.

I haven't been there for a long time.
It's only a visit.

Shoshanna invited me to her beach house.
Will I still have time to go?

I feel I might snap in two pieces,
one part of me here, one part in Jerusalem.

Sometimes wearing a hijab feels right.
Sometimes I want to wear my hair loose, like Shoshanna.

My sister says it's up to me. She understands.
I want to be both. Muslim, American.

She says I get to choose what is right for me.
I decide my sister is right.

The church smells too clean.
I feel like I can't breathe.
I escape to the back room,
where they've got donuts and coffee.
My brother finds me, fills a cup
halfway with milk, pours in some coffee.
I take small sips. Bitter and sweet.
The flavor makes me think of Grandpa,
his coffee breath in the morning.

I sit next to my brother in the pew,
but I imagine I am in my tree,
looking through the leaves at clouds,
until it seems I will fly upward
into a sea of sky, where Grandpa is waiting.
I touch the walnut turtle in my pocket,
tucked in there with my Tiger's Eye stone.
I don't know what it's going to be like
missing Grandpa. Every morning,
every day after school, he won't be here.

I see Norah, Rennie, and George at the church door,
coming up the aisle with Rennie's mom.
When our mothers hug, the girls hug me, too.
George bumps my fist. "You're here," I say.
George says, "Sure." They sit in the pew behind me.
I show them the turtle I made for Grandpa.

DREAM SCHOOL
Ben Kidwell

The teacher says,
"Come back to Earth, Ben."
I can't learn
sitting at a desk.
When they tear down this school
I hope they leave
a field
where new trees can grow.
I wish we had school
in the woods.
For classwork,
we could identify trees,
find box turtles, and
make recordings
of the spring frogs peeping.
The teacher says,
"Come back to Earth."
I must have been
staring out the window again,
thinking about
my dream school.

My mom has an old red dress
in the back of her closet.
She's been studying hard
for her degree.
She hasn't had time to dress nice
or even put on makeup.

My mom has a red dress.
She says it's too shabby
for interviews,
so she borrowed a gray suit
from her best friend.
When Mom told me and my brother
she got a job with Katie's mother,
I hid her old red dress under my bed.

My mom has a red dress.
I beaded the collar and fixed the hem.
She doesn't know it yet
but she's wearing it
to our Moving Up ceremony.
When I walk across the stage
I want to be able to see my mom.
She'll be easy to find
in her red dress.

May 13
••••••
TIME CAPSULE
Katie McCain

All year, I pictured
the time capsule
like this:

Silver rocket
blasting off.
Inside, our poems
are astronauts,
asleep in the dark,
waiting for
the ship to wake,
ready to make contact
with people
from the future.

I did not picture:

Plain old
dull metal box,
stuck behind a wall
inside the supermarket
my mom's helping
to build here
when our school
is torn down.

When fifth grade started,
I was sad.
A big part of my life was ending.
I couldn't believe anyone
would demolish this place.

When fifth grade started,
I was scared.
Certain people were mean.
I couldn't believe
the things they said to me.
Even though it was hard,
I learned to stand up for myself.

Now fifth grade is almost over.
I've been thinking,
what if we saved one wall?
One strong wall no bulldozers
can knock down.
One wall made of many bricks
held together, like our class.
We'll use it as a special place
to store the time capsule.
We can paint a mural
of all our faces.
One wall to say we were here.

TO MY TEACHER
Tyler La Roche

Dear Ms. Hill,

No matter what you say,
you are not too old
to start a new job
at a new school next fall.
Sure, your hair is gray,
but my mom says
you've still got a lot
of pep in your step.
Don't be afraid
of things changing.
I was nervous last summer
when we moved up north.
I didn't want to start
at a new school.
I thought people
would laugh at my accent
and I wouldn't make
any friends.

But I did, and even though
we didn't save this school,
fifth grade was the best
and you are my all-time
favorite teacher.
Think about it. Some poor kid
is packing up his house,
getting ready to move,
nervous about starting
fifth grade at a new school.
Please don't retire.
Out there, there's someone
like me who needs
a teacher like you.

May 18
• • • • • •
MOVING
Mark Fernandez

My family is moving.
My mom bought a new house
in Ohio so we can live
near my grandparents.

My sisters say they understand.
It's been hard for my mom
to live in our house,
always thinking of our Papi.

But I want to stay.
I don't need a change of scenery.
I need my friends.
I don't want new ones.

I want to stay where it's easy
to remember my father
packing up our tent, or
taking his bike out of the garage.

Finally, I get
why George tried so hard
to save our old school.
All our memories are here.

My mom says all my friends
will be starting over, just like me.
Everyone will make
new friends in middle school.

You're moving on, too, Ms. Hill.
Retiring when school ends.
That doesn't make me feel any better.
I am moving.

MR. STICK GUY'S GOODBYE
Jason Chen

For Mark

Find a pack of sticky notes.
Draw your old pal
Mr. Stick Guy.
On the next page
draw him a little smaller.
On the next page,
shrink him more.
Keep going,
smaller and smaller
on each page,
until he's nothing
but a dot.

Suddenly,
Other Stick Guy appears.
Draw a close-up
of his face.
Put a tear
in the corner
of his eye.
Make it roll
page by page
down his cheek.

Something good is going to happen this summer.
I can feel it. It's in the heat, the sun on my arms,
the way kids rush out the door
when school is over for the day.

Something good is going to happen this summer.
The pool is open. The water's cold.
My friends hang out by the snack shed,
talking about middle school.

Something good is going to happen.
Maybe my swim team will be county champs.
Maybe Mom will let me and Sloane go to the movies
by ourselves. Maybe I'll meet someone.

Something good is going to happen.
I can feel it in the way people don't ignore me
even when I'm with my sister.
That makes me feel like I'm something good.

PAINTING
Hannah Wiles

After lunch, Mrs. Stiffler says
we can spend the rest of the day
outside, painting our wall.

If I'm going to be a good
Holy Angels student,
I'd better start practicing now.
I guess I kind of
picked on Rachel this year.
So I tell her I am sorry
and how I think the mural
is a great idea. She looks shocked
that I gave her a compliment,
but Rachel and I work
next to each other all afternoon,
painting and talking.
I'm surprised! I never knew
Rachel was so easy to talk to.

Our class sings old folk songs
and laughs about the crazy things
that happened this year,
all eighteen of us and Ms. Hill,
having our own
fifth-grade celebration.

My sister and me
side by side on the mural.
Phoenix is smiling.
My hand holds her hand so tight,
no one can pull us apart.

Nobody told me
shutting down this school
meant Mrs. Stiffler would cancel
our Clapping Out ceremony.
Just because we're not
going to school here next year,
Mrs. Stiffler thinks it's pointless
to make the teachers applaud
while our class walks
between the buildings
and we officially
become middle schoolers.
Even though she gave us back
our fifth-grade celebration,
I think she's still mad at our class.
No teachers applauding
on our last day,
and no Hannah next year.
I'm thinking middle school
will be pointless ...
until Sydney reminds me
I won't be alone.
Lots of cool kids from our class
are going to Dickinson Middle.
But coolest of all is my
number one super friend
to the end,
sister Sydney.

I wanted to see my elementary school teachers lined up.
I wanted to feel my feet marching
    into Montgomery Middle.
I wanted my ears filled with the sound of teachers clapping.
I wanted the scent of middle-school lockers,
    emptied for the summer.
I wanted a taste of being a sixth grader.

Instead, I see my teachers packing boxes.
Instead, I feel dirt on the floor no one bothers to clean.
Instead, I hear the sound of people saying goodbye.
Instead, I smell the last lunch I will eat in this building.
Instead of celebrating our move to middle school,
    I'm surprised to taste my tears.

We saved the frog wall.
You're welcome, amphibians!
Your friends, Raj and Newt.

Finally, my dad
said I could play piano
with the Zoo Creatures.
My mask is a blue dart frog.
Wait till I tell Newt the news!

MY VOICE
Gaby Vargas

When fifth grade started,
I did not like my poems
unless I wrote them in Spanish.
But when Mark is helping me,
my English is getting better.

When fifth grade started,
I did not like my voice.
Too slow in English.
Clumsy, like dropping eggs.
But when I was singing
in the school play,
I loved being Belle.

Mark asked me to sing
with his band
at the picnic for the fifth grade.
Mark, Jason, Tyler,
Ben, Raj, and me
onstage together.
When I sing with my friends,
I like the sound of my voice.

Zoo Creatures
Onstage!
One last

Concert to
Rock
Emerson's fifth grade. Mark
And Gaby are at the mike.
Tyler, Jason, and Raj wait
Until I give the beat.
Ready
Everyone?
Showtime!

June 3
· · · · ·
UNVEILING THE MURAL
Norah Hassan

Brick wall, bright faces.
One girl in a blue hijab
smiles at her teacher.

Beside the children
a teacher stands tall, so proud.
Her scarf flutters, a flag.

When we dedicated the mural,
my mom nearly had a conniption.
She says people who go shopping
at the new supermarket won't know
what an awesome kid I am when they see
a painting of a girl with purple hair,
holding her pet snake.

At least Jason thinks I'm awesome,
no matter what color my hair is.
He asked my mom if I could go out
for ice cream after our Moving Up ceremony.
My mom said it was fine with her.
Me going out with Jason Chen.
What could be more normal?

MOVING UP SPEECH
Jason Chen

Dearly Exhausted,

We are gathered here to end
the many years we've spent together
at Emerson Elementary School.
Sickness—check. Health—check.
Better—sometimes.
Worse—let's not go there.
Forsaking all other fun activities
when there was homework to do?
Let's just say we did our best.

As we walk across this stage tonight,
fifth grade and Emerson
become memories
we shall have and hold
as long as we all shall live.
That means forever,
and that's a mighty long time,
but I'm here to tell you
there's something else—middle school.
A world of never-ending lockers,
where homework is assigned every night.
In this life, things have been much easier
than they are in middle school,
but take a look around you.
You won't be on your own.

By the power given to me
by the votes of my wise classmates
when they chose me to make this speech,
I now pronounce the fifth-grade class
Moved Up.

June 8
• • • • •
SELF-PORTRAIT
George Furst

Before the Moving Up ceremony,
I asked my father to come see our mural.
There I am on the wall.
My name is underneath:
George Washington Furst,
President of the Last Fifth Grade.

"Did you have a good year
as class president?" Dad asked.
I don't want to hurt his feelings.
I wish we could have saved Emerson
almost as much as I wish
I could have convinced my dad
to come home and live with me
and Mom and Vernon, the cat.

We look at the bulldozers,
already parked behind the school,
and I tell my dad
I'm running for student council
next year. One day, I hope to be
the student representative
to the Board of Education.
The kids in this school system
need a strong voice.
This year, I found mine.

GOODBYE
Edgar Lee Jones

Yo, Notebook.
Goodbye from your fifth-grade poet.
My class has Moved Up.
I wore a fine white suit,
black shirt, silver tie.
When I walked across the stage
I knew my mom would cry.
I am writing one last poem,
knowing my grandpa
is there, somewhere,
reading over my shoulder
never looking a day older.
I won't forget this year,
how we tried to keep
this building alive.
How fighting back
made our classroom thrive.

In twenty-five years,
when the time capsule
gets sprung from its wall,
I will take you out
and read all my poems
about friends, sad times,
things that made me
want to rhyme.
I know you'll be
waiting in the dark,
a quiet spark,
so I'll never forget
a fifth-grade boy
called Edgar Lee,
who loved poetry.

ACKNOWLEDGMENTS

According to the saying, it takes a village to raise a child. Imagine the size of the village required to bring Ms. Hill's eighteen students to life! I am grateful to many friends and readers, especially: Melinda Abbott, Marjory Bancroft, Veronica Bartles, Barbara Quarrier Dell, Jennifer Della'Zanna, Jacqueline Douge, Jane Elkin, Erin Hagar, Jennifer Dennison Lewis, Naomi Milliner, Marieke Nijkamp, Lona Queen, Debby Rippey, Amie Rose Rotruck, Holly Thompson, and Timanda Wertz. Joy McCullough-Carranza mentored me through a significant rewrite. Poet and translator Patricia Bejarano Fisher deserves recognition for her work on Gaby's poems. Hannah's poem "Hugs and Kisses" was inspired by the Hauk family. Thanks to the real Aunt Jennie, Jennie Steinhauser, for sharing her matzo candy. Ann Bracken and Patricia VanAmburg, educators and poets both, were models for Ms. Hill. Illustrator Abigail Halpin is so talented, I recognized each of the Emerson fifth graders immediately.

I could not have written this book without the Maryland State Arts Council's Artists-in-Residence Program. Among the classrooms I have visited, Northfield Elementary's third grade holds a special place in my heart.

The Last Fifth Grade and I found a champion in my amazing agent, Stephen Barbara, who is part coach, part expert guide to the ins and outs of publishing. Like me, Stephen is a fan of Edgar Lee Masters's 1915 verse novel, *Spoon River Anthology*, which was a model for early drafts.

It has been a joy working with the team at Wendy Lamb Books, whose time and energy enlivened Ms. Hill's class. I appreciate copy editor Colleen Fellingham's keen eye, and her patience. Art director Kate Gartner and senior designer Trish Parcell took great care to make *The Last Fifth Grade* feel as cozy as spending time with a good friend. Special thanks to my editor, Wendy Lamb, and her assistant, Dana Carey. They have been generous with their guidance, trust, and enthusiasm.

I am grateful for my children's patience and humor. And most humble thanks to my husband, Rob, who is not a writer, which makes his understanding that rarest of gifts: empathy.

A CLOSER LOOK
AT THE POEMS IN THIS BOOK

READING POETRY

The Last Fifth Grade of Emerson Elementary is a book of persona poems, which means that each poem is written in the voice of one of the characters.

Listen to those voices. Whether you are reading aloud or silently, imagine that these poems are no different from speaking with a friend. Poems are very much like people. They try to make you laugh with a joke, tell you a sad story, or share a secret. But like people, poems don't always reveal everything they know. You might want to ask the poem, "What do you mean when you say that?"

Sometimes the fun of reading a poem is laughing at silly rhymes like the ones Jason Chen writes. Other times the fun comes from creating pictures in your mind, like the ones described in Norah Hassan's poems. Best of all is when a poem hints at something that makes you want to figure out its meaning for yourself. Why is that the most fun? Because that is the moment when you become part of the poem.

FAVORITE FORMS FROM ROOM 5-H

Acrostic

In acrostic poems, the first letter of each line spells out the subject of the poem. This cool form is read the usual way, but also vertically, down the side of the page.

SUGGESTION: Write about a friend, using his or her name to form an acrostic. The more details you include about the person, the more your poem will resemble your friend.

Model poem: "Things That Annoy Me" by Katie McCain (page 86)

Concrete Poem

Concrete poems are shapely. The words of the poem form the shape of whatever the poem is about. We read the poem, but we also see it.

SUGGESTION: Pick an object that's important to you—your favorite soccer ball, a lucky hat, your pillow. Draw an outline of your object on paper. Fill in the shape by telling a story about your object, or describe what makes this item important to you.

Model poem: "Lucky Hat" by Ben Kidwell (page 26)

Diamante

Diamantes are seven-line poems. They are named for the diamond shape they make when centered on a page. Poets start with two nouns that are opposites ("Summer" and "Winter") or two words that are related ("Cold" and "Ice").

Line 1: Noun
Line 2: Two adjectives about the noun in line 1
Line 3: Three "-ing" verbs that show the noun in action
Line 4: Four nouns or a short phrase that link line 1 to line 7
Line 5: Three "-ing" verbs that show the last word of the poem in action
Line 6: Two adjectives about the noun in line 7
Line 7: Noun (synonym or antonym of line 1)

SUGGESTION: Write about a special day—a snow day, your birthday, or a holiday.

Model poem: "Valentine Diamante" by Rachel Chieko Stein (page 135)

Epistolary Poem

Epistolary means "written as a letter."

SUGGESTION: Make a poetry postcard. Draw a picture or cut out a photograph you like from a magazine and glue it on the front of your postcard. On the back, write a letter to someone (real or imaginary) in the form of a poem.

Model poem: "Anything" by Sydney Costley (page 80)

Fib (Fibonacci Poem)

Fibs are a new form of poem, invented by author Gregory K. Pinkus. By counting syllables, Fibs follow the Fibonacci sequence of numbers. It's easy to do. Start with 0 (an empty line). Then 1 (a one-syllable word). Add them together to get your next line: 0 + 1 = 1 syllable. Keep adding the last two numbers to get the next number in the sequence. In nature, Fibonacci numbers make a spiral like the ones formed in a nautilus shell. In a poem, the sequence looks like this:

Empty line: 0 syllables
Line 1: 1 syllable
Line 2: 0 + 1 = 1 syllable
Line 3: 1 + 1 = 2 syllables
Line 4: 1 + 2 = 3 syllables
Line 5: 2 + 3 = 5 syllables
Line 6: 3 + 5 = 8 syllables
Line 7: 5 + 8 = 13 syllables

SUGGESTION: Since the Fibonacci sequence is found in nature, try writing a Fib about the natural world. Insects and spiders, animals, plants, and even outer space all make great topics for Fibs.

Model poems: "Two Fibonacci Poems" by Newt Mathews (page 61)

Found Poem

Found poems were not originally meant to be poems. They can be grocery lists, homework assignments, or other scraps of writing. It's the poet who finds rhythm or imagery in a found poem. By rearranging the original writing, the poet can make the words look and sound like a poem.

SUGGESTION: Keep your eyes peeled! A found poem can come from anywhere: a sign describing a lost kitten, a famous speech, or a note from a friend.

Model poem: "My Speech" by George Furst (page 189)

Free Verse

In a free verse poem, the poet makes the rules. It's up to you whether your poem has stanzas, and whether the lines are long or short. Free verse poems do not usually rhyme or have a steady beat.

SUGGESTION: Do you have a story to tell? Free verse is the perfect form for a narrative poem. You don't have to think about rhyming words or counting syllables. Focus on describing your story.

Model poem: "Rennie and Phoenix" by Brianna Holmes (page 81)

Haiku

Haiku is a Japanese form of unrhymed poetry. Haiku describe scenes in nature. They include a *kigo* word, a symbol that lets the reader know what season the poet is writing about. You may have learned to count syllables when writing a haiku: 5-7-5. But Japanese is not written or read left to right, the way English is. Instead of counting syllables, aim for lines that have a short-long-short rhythm.

SUGGESTION: Go outside for a haiku hike. Take a notebook or index card with you and jot down a few things that you see. Then write about what you observed in lines with a short-long-short rhythm.

Model poems: "Two Haiku" by Newt Mathews (page 19)

Limerick

A limerick is a form poem most often used to tell a quick joke. Limericks have five lines with a rhyme scheme of AABBA. A rhyme scheme is the pattern of rhymes that appears in a poem. Each rhyming sound is assigned a different letter of the alphabet. In a limerick, the rhyme scheme looks like this:

A LIMERICK
There once was a girl named McCain, (A)
who sat next to someone insane. (A)
He thought it was cool (B)
to act like a fool, (B)
but his poems gave her a migraine. (A)

Limericks also have a rhythm of stressed and unstressed syllables. If you CLAP the stressed syllables and snap the unstressed syllables, it would sound like this:

Line 1: snap CLAP snap snap CLAP snap snap CLAP
Line 2: snap CLAP snap snap CLAP snap snap CLAP
Line 3: snap CLAP snap snap CLAP
Line 4: snap CLAP snap snap CLAP
Line 5: snap CLAP snap snap CLAP snap snap CLAP

SUGGESTION: Follow the form as best you can. If you're stuck, make it about a clumsy dinosaur who loves cherry lime soda (known as lime rickeys).

Model poem: "A Limerick" by Katie McCain (page 60)

List Poem

People have been making list poems for thousands of years. Lists are a great way to create a poem. Starting with a list makes the poet focus on objects or events instead of ideas. Many list poems use repetition, a word or phrase that emphasizes the theme of the list.

SUGGESTION: Try writing a list poem all about you. Stick to one topic, though, such as a list of things you collect, a list of places where you have been, a list of jobs you do NOT want when you grow up, a list of the pets you have had (or wished you had). A list poem can be about pretty much anything. The way you order the items is almost as important as the things on the list.

Model poem: "Top Ten Things That Stink When Your Father Dies" by Mark Fernandez (page 20)

Narrative Poem

Narrative poems tell a story or describe an event. They are often written in free verse.

SUGGESTION: In a poem, think about a time when you had to make a decision. Maybe you wanted to run for student council. Maybe you had to choose whether you wanted to give up soccer so you could try out for a dance company. Describe how you decided what to do.

Model poem: "News at the Newseum" by Sloane Costley (page 45)

Ode

Odes are poems of celebration that date back to ancient Greece, when poets would write verses praising Olympic champions. Modern poets use odes, which are usually written in free verse, to praise normal people, places, and objects. After all, your favorite aunt deserves just as much attention as a superstar athlete.

SUGGESTION: Write an ode to create a portrait—a picture in words—of someone with whom you are close, or to your favorite time of the school day. Use details to show the reader why a subject (any subject!) is so wonderful that it should be praised.

Model poem: "Ode to My Mom" by Rennie Rawlins (page 186)

Rap Poem

Like poets, rappers use rhythm and rhyme in their lyrics to get their point across. Rap poems often have short lines, which give the poem a quick rhythm. The rhymes might not always fall at the end of a line. Rap poems can be less formal and sound more like everyday speech than some other poems do.

SUGGESTION: Write a rap poem about a time when you really wanted something but didn't get it.

Model poem: "Time Capsule Rap" by Edgar Lee Jones (page 78)

Rhyming Poems

There are many ways for poems to rhyme. The most common are rhymed couplets (two rhymed lines), tercets (three rhymed lines), or quatrains (four rhymed lines). Rhymes can add humor to a poem.

SUGGESTION: Write a funny poem about homework using the rhyme scheme of your choice.

Model poem: "I Know This One" by Rajesh Rao (page 16)

Senryu

Senryu poems follow haiku form, but they do not have to be about nature. Often, senryu focus on human nature.

SUGGESTION: Write a description of yourself or someone else in senryu form.

Model poem: "Senryu: Shoshanna Says" by Rachel Chieko Stein (page 95)

Sonnet

The sonnet is a traditional form poem with fourteen lines. English (or Shakespearean) sonnets have a rhyme scheme of ABAB CDCD EFEF GG. Sonnets are sometimes used to make an argument.

SUGGESTION: In fourteen lines, tell a story about something that happened to you. You might need a special rhyming dictionary to help with the rhyme scheme.

CHALLENGE: Traditional sonnets use iambic pentameter, ten rhythmic beats per line, with an accent on every other syllable. Not easy, but fun to try.

Model poem: "Field Trip" by Edgar Lee Jones (page 44)

Tanka

Tanka is another form poem from Japan. The rules for tanka might remind you of haiku, with two extra lines.

An American tanka looks like this:

Line 1: 5 syllables
Line 2: 7 syllables
Line 3: 5 syllables
Line 4: 7 syllables
Line 5: 7 syllables

Because Japanese isn't written like English, it's more important to make the lines short/long/short/long/long than it is to count syllables. Tanka have two halves, the upper part (that looks like a haiku) and a lower part (the last long/long lines). Usually, the upper poem focuses on description and the lower poem adds a comment or observation.

SUGGESTION: Create a tanka portrait of someone you know. Use the first three lines to describe your person. Your senses will come in handy. What does your person look and sound like? Reserve the last two lines to make an observation about your subject. What does he want most in the world? What does she believe about herself?

Model poem: "Mr. White Tanka Poem" by Newt Mathews (page 37)

FROM THE FIFTH-GRADE POETRY PROMPT JAR

Start Making Sense

Write a poem about something you love, such as a sport, walking your dog, or a special memory. Try using all five senses to create imagery. Describe what you see, hear, feel, smell, and taste—whether you are playing football with your friends or geocaching with your family.

Model poem: "Spring Break Five Senses Poem" by Norah Hassan (page 175)

Food for Thought

Everybody eats! There are many ways to write a food poem. You can write a list poem about your favorite food using your five senses. You can write a recipe poem, describing how to make your favorite food. Or you can write a poem about a food tradition—a dish that your family shares on special occasions.

Model poem: "Marvelous Matzo" by Rachel Chieko Stein (page 176)

Happy Holidays/Hateful Holidays

Holidays make great topics for poetry. We get dressed up, sing and dance together, and have good things to eat. Write a poem about a holiday, but make sure it's specific. Tell a best or worst birthday story, or write a poem listing all the costumes you've ever worn on Halloween.

Sometimes holidays are a drag. There might be rules or traditions that you don't understand. People in your family might expect you to act a certain way. Write a poem about a holiday that wasn't so great, or one that you don't like.

Model poem: "I Hate Halloween" by Hannah Wiles (page 54)

A Sound Riddle

What if you wrote about a place using only the sounds you hear there? Would readers be able to guess where your poem is set? Imagine going to that place with a blindfold on (or go there for real and close your eyes for a few minutes). Focus on what you hear, then write it all down. To help your readers guess your place correctly, use onomatopoeia words—words that sound like the noise they describe.

Model poem: "Rainy Day Poem" by Ben Kidwell (page 156)

This or That?

Try writing an opposites poem with two stanzas. Your poem can describe "Before and After" or "Then and Now." It could also be about opposites like "Summer and Winter" or "Home and School."

CHALLENGE: Use rhyme to make your poem funny.

Model poem: "Time Capsule" by Katie McCain (page 204)

Parody

Something funny happened to you at school today and you want to write about it. But simply telling the story feels a little ho-hum. Try a parody! Take a few lines from a favorite book or song. Rewrite the words to fit your story. This might not look like a poem when you are done. That's okay. Dramatic—or comedic—dialogue has a lot in common with poetry.

Model poem: "One Seat, Two Seats, We Have New Seats" by Jason Chen (page 59)

Personification Poem

Instead of writing a poem about an object, write *to* an object. This is called using direct address. Choose anything you like for this poem: a window, a dust bunny, your sister's cell phone, the silver dragon on your best friend's bookshelf. Act as if that object is your new buddy and write a note to it. If you're stuck, try writing to the pen or pencil you're using. What words might be stuck in there?

CHALLENGE: Instead of writing to the object you are personifying, let it speak for itself. What would your backpack complain about if it could talk?

Model poem: "Notebook" by Edgar Lee Jones (page 3)

Picture This

Write about a photograph you love. It can be a funny photo, a picture of someone you care about, or of a special place you've been to or dream of visiting someday. Include specific details about the photograph, such as who is in it, what else you see in the picture, and where it was taken. Write down all the things you can see in your photograph, but also tell why it's important to you.

Model poem: "Photograph" by Edgar Lee Jones (page 99)

Paint a Portrait

We usually think about portraits as works of art, such as paintings or photographs. But we can also make portraits of people with words. Write a poem describing your favorite teacher or coach or your oldest friend. Include details to show what made—or makes—that person so great. Did she play flag football with you at recess? Did he shake your hand every morning or help you learn your favorite pop song on the piano?

Model poem: "To My Teacher" by Tyler La Roche (page 206)

Routine Description

Think about something you do every day. Do you rush out the door every morning, or wake up early and get things done? Write a free verse poem describing a routine. Brainstorm by listing everything you do before school, or while getting ready to play a sport. Once you have a list, pick a few things that seem interesting. Spend a few lines describing each item.

Model poem: "Every Morning" by Norah Hassan (page 13)

Recess

Describe your favorite thing to do at recess. A game, a sport, or talking with friends? Try using short lines for this poem. Short lines give a poem a fast rhythm, and we all know recess goes by too fast.

Model poem: "Crack the Whip" by Sloane Costley (page 90)

Mirror, Mirror

Write an "I Am" self-portrait poem. Think of each stanza as a paragraph with its own main idea. Begin each stanza with the phrase "I am": "I am shoulder pads and a football helmet," "I am hands that sign words," "I am recipes of my own invention." The more detailed images your poem has, the better your readers will get to know who you are.

Model poem: "School Clothes" by Brianna Holmes (page 8)

The Story of My (Nick)Name

Have you ever asked where your name comes from? Names are part of who we are. They can connect us with our family history. What's the story of your name or nickname? Was there ever a time when you didn't like your name? What do you like about it? Tell the story of your name.

Model poem: "My Song" by Tyler La Roche (page 40)

"Stream-of-Consciousness" Poem

In stream-of-consciousness writing, the author writes down everything that comes into her mind. Sit down and write whatever pops into your brain, no matter how wacky it is. Don't try to fix or edit as you write. After a page or a paragraph of writing, put your poem away for a few days. When it's time to revise, read what you wrote and highlight parts you like. See if you can build a poem from those highlighted bits.

Model poem: "Ping-Pong Riff" by Jason Chen (page 12)

You Are What You Wear

Write about your favorite piece of clothing—a lucky shirt, a pair of jeans you've graffitied with colored pens, or your favorite fuzzy socks. What makes that thing special to you?

CHALLENGE: Try a concrete poem. Shape your poem so it looks like the piece of clothing you're writing about.

Model poem: "Lucky Hat" by Ben Kidwell (page 26)

GLOSSARY

alliteration: A repeated sound at the beginning of successive words.

assonance: A repeated vowel sound.

couplet: Two lines, either a poem or a stanza within a poem, usually with rhyming end words.

descriptive details: Specific elements and language used to create a vivid picture.

direct address: Speaking to a person or an object.

form poem: A poem that has rules, such as a specific number of lines (e.g., a sonnet), a certain rhythm or rhyme scheme (e.g., a limerick), or even a particular subject (e.g., a haiku).

iambic pentameter: A line of poetry with five pairs of beats. In each pair, the second syllable is accented (e.g., snap CLAP in the entry on limericks).

imagery: Pictures created by using certain words. All five senses can be used to create imagery.

internal rhyme: Rhymes that appear in places other than at the end of a line.

kigo: A word or phrase that symbolizes a season; used in Japanese poetry.

meter: The rhythmic pattern of a poem.

near rhyme: Also called "slant rhyme." When two words don't rhyme perfectly.

onomatopoeia: Words that sound like the noise they are describing.

parody: A funny imitation of another work of art.

personification: Giving an animal or object human qualities.

poetic form: The rules that a poem follows, such as rhyme scheme or number of syllables.

prompt: A poem starter, a character or setting suggestion for a short story, or an idea for free writing.

quatrain: A four-line poem or stanza. It can be unrhymed or rhymed.

repetition: Using a specific word or phrase multiple times to emphasize an idea or make a point.

rhyme scheme: The pattern of rhymes in a poem.

rhythm: The beat that a poem's words make.

stanza: Two or more lines of a poem grouped together.

syllables: The units of sound in a word. Some form poems have a required number of syllables. Poets often pay attention to which syllables are stressed (heavier beat) and unstressed (lighter beat).

tercet: A three-line poem or stanza. Tercets can be rhymed AAA or ABA, or they can be unrhymed.

theme: The main subject.

ABOUT THE AUTHOR

LAURA SHOVAN has been a writer since the second grade, when her short story "Snow Flurry" appeared in a PTA newsletter. After graduating from NYU's Dramatic Writing Program, she taught high school, worked as a freelance journalist, and is now an educational consultant for teens with learning differences. Laura is the editor of two poetry anthologies and author of the Harriss Poetry Prize—winning chapbook, *Mountain, Log, Salt, and Stone.* She and her family live in Maryland, where Laura is a longtime poet-in-the-schools for the Maryland State Arts Council. This is her first novel.